MARKET ST. PARKERSBURG, W. VA.

COLUMBIA,
MO.

Finding Family

Finding Family

Tonya Bolden

BLOOMSBURY

NEW YORK BERLIN LONDON

The photographs used in this book are from the author's private collection. Although the author and publisher have made extensive efforts to identify the photographers of these photos, they have been unable to do so beyond what is attributed here. They are historical photographs of real people, though their identities are unknown to the author or publisher. They bear no resemblance to characters in this book apart from physical descriptions. The characters are wholly imagined by the author. Should you recognize a photo—perhaps one of your own family!—we'd love to know about it. Please write to us through the author's Web site, www.tonyaboldenbooks.com.

First published in the United States of America in September 2010
by Bloomsbury Books for Young Readers
www.bloomsburykids.com

For information about permission to reproduce selections from this book, write to Permissions, Bloomsbury BFYR, 175 Fifth Avenue, New York, New York 10010

"I Thirst" taken from *Sketches of Southern Life* by Frances E. Watkins Harper, Philadelphia: Ferguson Bros. & Co., 1891

Library of Congress Cataloging-in-Publication Data
Bolden, Tonya.
Finding family / by Tonya Bolden. — 1st U.S. ed.
p.   cm.
Summary: Raised in Charleston, West Virginia, at the turn of the twentieth century by her grandfather and aunt on off-putting tales of family members she has never met, twelve-year-old Delana is shocked when, after Aunt Tilley dies, she learns the truth about her parents and some of her other relatives.
ISBN 978-1-59990-318-7
[1. Families—Fiction. 2. Self-perception—Fiction. 3. Grandfathers—Fiction.
4. Aunts—Fiction. 5. Secrets—Fiction. 6. African Americans—Fiction. 7. West Virginia—History—20th century—Fiction.] I. Title.
PZ7.B635855Fi 2010   [Fic]—dc22   2010000535

Book design by Danielle Delaney
Typeset by Westchester Book Composition
Printed in the U.S.A. by Worldcolor Fairfield, Pennsylvania
2 4 6 8 10 9 7 5 3 1

All papers used by Bloomsbury Publishing, Inc., are natural, recyclable products made from wood grown in well-managed forests. The manufacturing processes conform to the environmental regulations of the country of origin.

In memory of my father
Willie James Bolden
February 19, 1933–September 18, 2009

Finding Family

Prologue

I was five, maybe six, the very first time I laid eyes on a dragonfly—spellbound by its magical dazzle. From then on, whenever I saw dragonflies, I got as close as I could, making merry in my mind over their shimmershine—red, blue, copper, green.

All I had was fairy tale thoughts, fancying dragonflies, like butterflies, jewelry for the sky.

My jumping-jack joy for dragonflies dimmed, then died, after Aunt Tilley told me some folks call them the Devil's darning needles.

That night I had the worst nightmare of my life.

I was cuddled up in the porch swing, eyes closed against a setting sun, when, suddenly, I felt a fluttering around my face, then dragonflies sewing up my lids. I tried to scream—they started stitching shut my lips.

After that dream, I never closed my eyes when dragonflies were near—and kept my distance. Always would, I reckoned. But little did I know, when I was twelve, that a change was coming as touched on dragonflies. And everything else in my world.

One

Y ou have six toes?" spat Viola Kimbrough.

This was in the school yard during recess on what was, till then, a peaceable early September day.

Viola was standing right over Adena Mullins when she asked about her toes.

Adena was on her haunches, drawing something in the dirt.

I say "something" because I was off a ways by myself at the picnic table, keeping neat, being meek as a lamb, like Aunt Tilley told me good girls were to be.

Nothing meek about Viola. Vicious to the bone.

"I asked you a question." Viola stamped her foot. "Six toes. Yes or no?"

Adena kept drawing.

I wished I had it in me to tell Viola to leave Adena alone. I felt bad for her, especially as Adena was so new to our school. The Mullins family hadn't been in Charleston long, with Adena's pa working the seasons and her ma taking in laundry and selling handicrafts. Adena helped out on pickups and deliveries.

"Take off your shoes!" Viola was louder now. Meaner, too. She shoved Adena, then hollered for other Kimbroughs—"Macey! Charlie! Hold her down!"

Next, Viola whipped around, eyes daggerlike at me. "Dumb Delana, get over here and take off Adena's shoes!"

Lawdamercy! All of me trembled. I could hear my heart thump-thumping. My stomach did a churn.

"Viola! Macey! Charlie!"

That was our teacher, Miss Tolliver, in the doorway. Her eyes said a soft "there, there" when she glanced at Adena, then at me, but they were like stone as she beckoned the three Kimbroughs inside.

I didn't expect Viola and her cousins to get punished much. Viola's father was the richest colored man in the county—and the school's Santa

Claus, giving more than even Grandpa. Mr. Kimbrough had just presented our principal everything the school needed to have a brass band, from a tuba to a big, boom-boom bass drum.

Thump-thumping. My heart was still thump-thumping though the Kimbroughs were gone from the yard. I said a silent *Thank you, Father God!* for Miss Tolliver. She had come just in the nick of time. Not just for Adena's sake. Miss Tolliver had been my rescue, too.

Truth be told, in that split second between Viola's command and Miss Tolliver's "Viola, Macey, Charlie!" I was in a terrible tug-of-war—yanked to turn my back on Viola, yanked to do her bidding. Maybe then she'd stop picking on me.

Thanks to Miss Tolliver, I was spared having to choose.

- - - - -

Still, that tug-of-war kept pricking me, like on the afternoon, a few days later, when Aunt Tilley up and remarked that I had a "spacious mind."

I started to cry. I thought it was a way of calling me a fool, dumb, or something else bad—like Viola Kimbrough did me.

Dumb Delana, get over here and take off Adena's shoes!

Aunt Tilley must have felt me well up.

"Oh no, Delana, don't cry! I'm telling you about your *blessing*! You are a child of promise!" Then she gave me her sunshine smile.

We were out on the back porch. Aunt Tilley and Grandpa in rockers by the door. Me off to the side in the swing.

As was our Sunday custom, we had come outside after dinner to "behold Creation." That's how Aunt Tilley put it.

I was beholding a horde of dragonflies. They were hovering around the blue hydrangea, moving back and forth, side to side.

At first, it seemed Aunt Tilley was looking at the dragonflies, too, but it was more like she was staring *through* them as she talked on about me being a child of promise and how she named me Delana because we are kin to Martin Delany.

"He was born over up in Jefferson County, back when there was just one Virginny. There was no West Virginia like we live in now."

I'd learned all about the making of West Virginia in school. About Martin Delany, too, but the most I remembered clear was that he'd started the first newspaper for our people out this way. *The Mystery* was its name. Now that I knew he was kin, my mind perked up.

Aunt Tilley was all het up for me to remember *everything* about Martin Delany as she raced on about how he was a doctor, wrote books, went to Africa in search of a ripe place for colored people to live, then changed his mind when the Civil War broke out. He joined the Union army.

"First of our race to make *major*—and on Father Abraham's say-so!" Aunt Tilley saluted the strange and sultry air. "Knew if I named you Delana, you'd make the family proud like Martin did."

Grandpa twisted up his face like he wished Aunt Tilley would hush, then hung his head when she didn't.

"Right along with his Missus, Martin Delany had high hopes for their children. Give them names to point the way!" Aunt Tilley exclaimed, then went to squinting like she was sorting through a tin of tiny buttons.

"Now, Tilley," Grandpa sighed, "that's enough about Martin Delany. No need to go on with this."

Aunt Tilley kept searching her mind.

"Alexander Doomas!" she finally cried out, smacking her lips in satisfaction. "That's what the Delanys named one son. Another one . . . after that great Haiti man—Two Cent!"

The dragonflies were still doing a dance with me keeping top-eye open should they swarm nearer to the house.

The screen door shut. Grandpa had gone inside. To the sitting room, I guessed. To play checkers with himself.

Aunt Tilley didn't seem to notice Grandpa had left. "Other children," she mumbled, face all frantic and scratching her head, "Lawdamercy . . . names on the run."

After a long silence, Aunt Tilley asked, "Picked what you'll stitch next?" like needlework had been the course of conversation all along.

"No'm." I knew she'd pick no matter what I thought.

"Pink primrose be nice."

"Yes'm."

When I glanced again at the hydrangea, I saw the dragonflies hover up, then dart away.

Two

"Time for needlework!"

Aunt Tilley was getting more and more twitchy, flitting from thing to thing.

I had been up in my room, practicing cursive like she told me, when she hollered up the stairs.

So I put my pen down and headed to the sitting room, where we always did our needlework: me having to embroider hankies, her only making doilies lately.

Rounds, squares, rectangles, ovals. Long, short. For dressers, bureaus, tables. For chair and sofa backs. Aunt Tilley made those doilies so fast—sometimes four, five a day—like she was in a doily-making race and the prize was her life.

Aunt Tilley had even started coming to breakfast with her hook and yarn, forsaking all food and only taking coffee, then letting that get cold as all she did was talk and crochet.

On the afternoon she called me away from my cursive, I took my place on the sitting room sofa and started stitching. She still had me doing primroses. Periwinkle this time.

But not for long. Before the clock chimed, Aunt Tilley put down her hook and yarn, eyed me to do likewise with my needle and thread, then yelled, like a house afire, "Time to visit kinfolk!" as she reached behind the sofa for the basket atop the sewing table.

That's where she kept the kinfolk now.

These photographs used to be across the hall in the parlor, on the big lion's paw table behind the red velvet settee. The tintypes and the pictures Aunt Tilley called "card visits" had been in a little leather album. The bigger portraits, in a keepsake box.

Used to be we visited kinfolk maybe once a year. And the visits were brief. All Aunt Tilley did back then was point to a picture and say something simple.

Like a name—"They the Dowds."

Or a name plus a tidbit—"Cousin Clare, she's still up in Parkersburg . . . Uncle Matthias, down in Madison."

Back then, she hardly ever told me if a kinfolk was blood or married-in. One time she did was when she pointed at the woman with a long cross and a yonder gaze.

"Aunt Viney. Evangelist. Me and your grandpa's sister."

After Aunt Tilley got all twitchy, visiting kinfolk was far from simple. It became a big to-do.

With the basket of pictures on one arm, Aunt Tilley marched me from the sitting room and across the hall into the parlor. There, she put a different handful of family on display—mantel, settee, windowsills, wherever she felt they fit best. After she had everybody just so, she had us stroll, arm in arm, around the room.

Sometimes Aunt Tilley talked to a photograph— like "Howdy!" or "Good day!"

Sometimes she spurned a person, muttering the likes of "floozy" or "danger-life!" at their picture.

Most amazing of all, Aunt Tilley had started giving me so much more than tidbits about kinfolk.

On the day Aunt Tilley put Aunt Viney on the

mantel, I learned she and her long cross lived on the road, sleeping at a follower's home in whatever town she had a camp meeting. And she walked *everywhere*. Never took a train. Never rode a buggy.

On another day, when Uncle Matthias was propped up in a side chair, I learned he'd traveled all around the nation as a railroad porter.

"Knowledgeable about hundreds of cities." Aunt Tilley tapped her temple. "A human telegraph, too! Take a message here, deliver it there. Always generous with information and news." Her eyes darted around the room, then went narrow. "About other matters, I have my doubts," she whispered. "I never let myself forget ole Matthias have a wily eye."

Just like the dog he posed with in the picture, I thought.

The day Aunt Tilley had me put aside my periwinkle primrose, Cousin Eula was the feature.

Aunt Tilley sighed when she picked up Eula from the baseboard.

I smiled at Eula. I liked how she was framed in the oval and how it was edged with dainty leaves looking as if time had stopped amid a cool-breeze sway.

"Eula came to a tragic end in Pittsburgh."

"How did she die?" I asked.

Aunt Tilley dropped Eula's picture, flopped in the armchair, rolled her eyes, lollygagged her tongue, shook like she was having a fit, then froze and said opera-like, "Oh, she died like this!"

I laughed so hard I got a stitch in my side.

Hadn't meant to trigger Aunt Tilley's new game, but next thing I knew I wanted to ask how somebody else died, because I wanted to laugh again and for us to keep playing "Oh, she died like this!"

Without meaning to, I thought about my mother, something I wasn't supposed to do. And we never played the game about her. Or about anybody else real, only made-up people from storybooks.

Till now.

Grandpa said we shouldn't play it at all. "Unseemly." That's what I'd overheard him mumble to our housekeeper, Ida Nash. Then he added something about Aunt Tilley "and her foolishness coming like a crop."

Aunt Tilley had told me all we had to do was make the sign of the cross after we laughed and Father God wouldn't mind our game. I didn't understand how that would work. We weren't Catholic.

Still, I crossed myself as I picked Eula up off the floor.

Miss Pearle Bruce
With best regards from
Emma Smith

"Fell down a long flight of mansion stairs. That's how Eula died." Aunt Tilley was back to sitting normal in the armchair. "Broke neck, broke back."

That wasn't funny. *How awful*, I thought as I sat down on the floor by Aunt Tilley's side. "Somebody pushed her—a bandit out to steal all the silver?"

Aunt Tilley waved her hand. "Tripped.... This here picture the last we seen of her after she decided to live a lie." Aunt Tilley's glance said, *I don't want to say but I want you to ask.*

I idled on why else I liked Eula's picture. She looked like she was top boss of her world. I wondered what that felt like.

"Truth will out," muttered Aunt Tilley.

I still didn't ask about Eula living a lie.

"Shoulda known not to have a child. Soon as her Mister saw their baby browner than two white folks could make ... If he wasn't a powerful white man—banker—he'd a been strung up."

So now I knew why Aunt Tilley didn't shine to Eula. Eula had gone passing—left the race and declared herself a white lady.

But I didn't understand the other part. "Aunt Tilley, why you say her husband would've hanged if he wasn't powerful?"

"Threw the baby out the window! Choked Eula to death!"

I was even more confused. "You said she fell down mansion stairs—tripped."

Aunt Tilley's nostrils flared.

I looked away. She didn't like to be stared at when collecting her thoughts. Worse, her faraway gaze had me scared. More so after I took a hard look at Eula's photograph.

It was stamped Des Moines, not Pittsburgh. The message on the back bewildered me, too.

Had Eula changed her name to Emma?

And who was Pearlie Bruce?

Three

How did she die?
Something inside her thought almost-December was July, I guess.

Had I not been such a heavy sleeper . . .

Our rooms were side by side. I would have heard the floorboards creak, peeked out my door, said, "Aunt Tilley, what you doing up?"

If she didn't answer, I would have hurried down to The Traveler's Room and shaken Grandpa awake.

Aunt Tilley wouldn't have left the house in a nightshirt and straw hat, all mixed up about night and day.

She was found down by the Kanawha, leaning against a tree.

That's what I heard Miss Ida say. She was in the kitchen with some neighbor ladies come to pay respects and ask what could they do to help with the funeral and all.

Sounded like Miss Ida was about to speak more on how Aunt Tilley died, when she switched to talking about bread pudding. She must've heard me breathing on the other side of the kitchen door.

I tiptoed away, through the dining room and into the sitting room. All I could think to do was visit kinfolk. Pick through the basket. Wonder who'd be coming and if I'd know them right off. Most of the photographs were old.

Next thing I knew, snippets of kinfolk stories were swooping and swirling in my head.

Oh, he was one smart . . .

Mind like a sieve, she had . . .

Suffered for years but then . . .

Glory to Father God, the lost was found!

I saw the faces Aunt Tilley made. How she sucked her teeth. Or winked. Or frowned. The way she saved her sunshine smile for favorite kin.

I was trying so hard to be strong, to not cry, even though Grandpa wasn't home.

Earlier that morning, when he was up in my room telling me Aunt Tilley was gone, I started to cry, but then stopped when Grandpa told me to be strong.

All I wanted was for him to hug me, but he just patted me on the back, jingling change in his pocket, like he always did when out of sorts.

"Won't do you no good to work yourself up into a state," Grandpa said as he left my room. "Be strong."

Be strong. That's what I kept telling myself as I sat in the sitting room with the kinfolk. I didn't want Grandpa to see my eyes all red and puffy when he returned from the telegraph office, letting family know Aunt Tilley was dead.

I still couldn't believe it. Aunt Tilley was dead?

Soon as I heard Miss Ida say they'd found her down by the Kanawha against a tree, I was sure Aunt Tilley had died at her wishing-place, where she always went to say her dreams. She never took me there, only said it was down by the river beneath a welcoming tree.

Under that tree was where she and Uncle Dub had their first picnic. And that very day, she wished him to be her husband. After that came true, she always went down to her secret place to wish on things of "holy specialness," like a child of strong body and mind when she knew she was in the family way. Sure enough, their son, Richard, was a wish come true—strong body, strong mind.

Years later, she'd gone down by the Kanawha to wish for love more bountiful when she knew she'd be the one to mother me.

By then, Uncle Dub was with the Lord and Aunt Tilley living in this house with Grandpa. And Cousin Richard, he was away at Storer College with a pocketful of plans that would take him to Pennsylvania. To Huntingdon. That's where his sweetheart Cora was from and where Grandpa staked him in a printing shop.

Whenever Aunt Tilley told me about Grandpa helping her son get his start in life, she said Grandpa would have helped Richard if he wasn't his nephew. "Your grandpa always been a good judge of character. No industrious young fella ever had to ask twice for his help."

- - - - -

Cousin Richard got here as soon as he could, and looking so tired from all the hours spent on one

train or another. But no amount of tired could hide his handsome.

It had been a while since he'd paid a visit. I'd forgotten that he wasn't as severe as he looked in his pictures. Close to mean in the last one.

"His simpleton of a wife couldn't even see to his tie being straight," Aunt Tilley had complained. Seemed to me it was the photographer who should have told him to fix it. Too, Cousin Cora didn't look like a simpleton to me. Sharp as a tack, she seemed.

And she was in the family way again. That's what I heard Cousin Richard explain when Grandpa saw him up to the room Miss Ida had readied for him. Of the four bedrooms upstairs, it was the only one that didn't have walnut or oak furniture. Instead, every piece, from bed and bureau to trinket mirror on the dressing table—all the furniture was sandy white with glimmers of gold. And the wallpaper was like a song. Big purple maypops in a whimsy.

I'd always figured that room had been my mother's, but never dared ask. Aunt Tilley got so flustery whenever she caught me peeking in there.

But that room wasn't on my mind the evening Cousin Richard arrived. Aunt Tilley's was. During supper, I asked Grandpa if I could sleep in her room.

Miss Ida had just served the corn soup.

"Might give you nightmares." That's how Grandpa said "No."

"But—"

"Finish your soup."

While Grandpa frowned, Cousin Richard gave me a smile. More glorious than even his mother's sunshine smile. Suddenly, he was the most handsome man in the world. I wanted to run down to the Kanawha, find myself a wishing-place, and ask Father God to still be making handsome men when I get grown. And good men, I would add. Men who don't run off like my father.

Cousin Richard would never do a thing like that. And I was sure he wouldn't mind at all if I made a remembrance for Aunt Tilley on her bedroom door. But, Grandpa, he'd just say no.

So I made that remembrance in my mind between spoonfuls of corn soup.

- - - - -

What I imagined on Aunt Tilley's door was a big black velvet bow and, in the center, her favorite photograph of herself. It was from the time she went to Huntingdon, when Richard and Cora had their first baby, James. While Aunt Tilley was in Pennsylvania, Richard took her to see kin in York.

"For no rhyme or reason my dear Richard bought me a hat!" That hat had what Aunt Tilley called "a white festivity." She couldn't wait to get her picture taken.

"That photography place was beehive busy and them Shadle and Busser people had all kinds of scenery," she'd told me. "You could get a picture of yourself at a mountainside or with sailboats in the distance. You could pose with a book, touching a table."

Aunt Tilley got all big-eyed when she told me about a chair that brought to mind a throne. "Perfect match for the hat my dear Richard give me!"

She gave me a sunshine smile, a smile I'd never see again, a smile I wanted to believe she had on when she went down to the Kanawha that one last time. To make a wish. Under the welcoming tree.

After I made that remembrance in my mind, I was thinking Aunt Tilley ought to be buried in her white festivity hat, but I knew better than to interrupt Cousin Richard and Grandpa's talk about taxes, suppliers, rates, and such.

So I finished my soup, hankering to know Aunt Tilley's last wish and wondering, *Who will mother me now?*

Four

I said "No!" to Cousin Mahala. Lawdamercy, I sure didn't want her to be the one. May she stay in Boston, I prayed.

That's what I was thinking after Grandpa and Cousin Richard left to take their coffee in the parlor and I was helping Miss Ida clear the dining room table.

Earlier, I'd overheard Miss Ida tell Grandpa there was no end to women kin who would be happy to come finish where Aunt Tilley left off with me.

Mahala's was just one of the photographs that popped up in my mind. She looked the type to fuss a lot and I didn't want somebody fussy taking care of me.

Until Grandpa made his pick, I supposed he'd have Miss Ida come every day for whole days. She'd like that, I was sure. She seemed sweet on Grandpa. Better, she never acted like I was a bother. Even slipped me a piece of candy now and then. And sometimes she seemed downright interested in me, as me.

If I was watching her make a mess of greens, frying fish, or polishing the silver, she asked me questions. Not like she was checking up on me, the way Aunt Tilley did, but like she was just curious.

The more I thought about it, the more I hoped Grandpa would have Miss Ida be full-time *and* have an aunt or cousin move in. Then I wondered, *What if I had some say?*

After I scraped the tablecloth for crumbs, I slipped into the sitting room, took the basket of kinfolk from atop the sewing table and up to my room.

- - - - -

I fished out Mahala first.

I had remembered right. Too fussy-like.

I said "No!" to Mahala again.

But "Yes!" to Aunt Rachel, never mind that Aunt

DIAMOND STUDIO.
54 TREMONT ROW
BOSTON.

Tilley sucked her teeth and muttered "floozy" at her picture.

I liked the way Aunt Rachel decorated herself. She had the same sense about her as Eula. Top boss of her world!

And I was so hoping Aunt Tilley had mixed Eula up with somebody else. I wanted her name to be Emma, like was on the back of her photograph. "Emma" sounded more bouncy.

Above all, may she not be passing. Or dead. That way when she came for the funeral she'd tell me all about her life as an opera singer or something lively like that, something that had her traveling around the world, but now she was tired, so tired. Tired of crossing oceans. Tired of keeping up with hatboxes and steamer trunks. She was ready to stay put where she had family. Like Charleston, West Virginia. Then I'd say "Yes!" to Emma.

I could see Aunt Tilley up in Heaven hollering "Yes!" to Cousin Clare.

I'd forgotten how she was kin, but I remembered Cousin Clare always rated placement on the parlor mantel or the lion's paw table. That's because she was a teacher. With her, I'd end up double-smart, but never laugh again, I feared. She

DUPLICATES OF THIS MAY BE HAD AT ANY TIME FROM THE GALLERY.

Loomis

Cor Market & 7ᵗʰ Sts.
PARKERSBURG W.Va.

always brought to mind stories about damsels in distress. So weepy! My stomach hurt every time I looked at her.

Under her picture was that of Cousin Amber-tine. She had grown up here, down the street. And blood kin, I knew. Her pa was Grandpa and Aunt Tilley's older brother, Jake, another one dead, like his wife, Mamie.

Aunt Tilley would have a fit if I said "Yes!" to Ambertine.

"Trash and trouble!" That's what she muttered when we strolled by Ambertine down on a baseboard.

Ambertine had been wild. She had run away. To join the circus—that's what I figured the first time I saw the photograph of her in a beehive-busy black dress and a hat like something from an Ali Baba tale.

But then, when Aunt Tilley told me Ambertine made her money off other people's miseries, I wondered if Ambertine was a thief. I could see her swinging and swacking at people with that umbrella.

"Sold her soul to the Devil for filthy lucre!" Aunt Tilley also said of Ambertine. "Night and day from Wade."

Wade was Ambertine's brother, a doctor in Washington, D.C. "He made the family proud," Aunt Tilley said of Wade.

He sure looked like he was bound and

determined to make the family—the whole world—proud, but what I most liked about his picture was seeing "Charleston" printed so pretty at the bottom. When I was younger, I hadn't been able to make out the word on the other side.

"Gates," Aunt Tilley had said. "That's the name of the photographer. Down on Capitol Street."

No telling where Ambertine's picture was taken. The more I looked at her, the more I wondered if she truly was nothing but trash and trouble. Up close, she looked a little lonely and like she might have a hiding kindness.

Maybe Ambertine had changed, turned from her wild ways. For all I knew, she could have given the Devil back his filthy lucre, whatever that was.

- - - - -

Seemed I'd never find out, though. Ambertine didn't come to Aunt Tilley's funeral. Neither did Mahala or Rachel. No Emma who I hoped wasn't Eula, either. But Cousin Clare came, mostly gray and still looking weepy.

Uncle Matthias was *all* gray. Stooped, too. Only when he called me to him—"Who you?" Then I knew. He still had the wily eye.

His dog, I guessed, had died.

Cousin Clare and Uncle Matthias were just the first family I met. Others came from Bluefield, Cucumber, and other places I could only wonder about. I'd never been nowhere.

Some kin who lived far or were feeble sent telegrams and cards. Miss Ida made a nice display of them on the hall table. That's where she also laid the guest book for relatives and townsfolk to sign.

Of all who came, the biggest surprise was Aunt Viney, the woman who walked the world.

I recognized her long cross right off, but not the rest of her. Face so shriveled. Hair white-white, but she still had a bit of bangs. And though she must have been a hundred years old, Aunt Viney wasn't decrepit. That I could see clear from up on the landing. She stood soldier-straight in the front doorway and had a tight grip on a beat-up leather bag like doctors carry.

But how did she know?

A whipping wind swept in as Aunt Viney told how she came to be on our doorstep the night before Aunt Tilley's funeral.

"Was up in Ohio, Ashtabula County, tilting toward Maine. The Holy Spirit said, 'Go south, Viney, go south.' At the West Virginia border, same thing— 'Go south, Viney, go south.' Soon as I set foot in Hebron, it wasn't no longer the Holy Spirit speaking. 'Twas Tilley. 'Come see me, Viney, come see me.'"

A shiver went through me. But it wasn't the cold.

Aunt Viney was all the way inside by then. Grandpa had closed the door. Miss Ida had taken her bag.

I wondered if the shiver was some of the Holy Spirit sparking off Aunt Viney. She sure looked like the holiest person in the world. Still so much yonder in her eyes.

And there was so much kindness in Cousin Richard's—in all of him. What with the other bedrooms spoken for, like the cots set out in the sitting room, Cousin Richard insisted Aunt Viney have the room he was in. Said he'd be just fine with a pallet in the library.

Cousin Richard was so nice to me, too. From one of his trips to Capitol Street, he brought me back a huge bag of candy! Brittle and jelly beans, Hershey bars, lots of lollipops, Tootsie Rolls. Lemon drops, too. I'd never seen so much candy.

"This all for me?"

"Yes, my dear Delana." He smiled. "All for you!"

Aunt Tilley had only let me have candy once in a blue moon. Said too much would curdle my mind. Cousin Richard didn't think candy was bad for me—or him, I learned when I helped him tote his things down to the library. I held my candy bag open to him, and he took a whole handful.

He popped jelly bean after jelly bean into his mouth as he swiveled in the chair before the roll-top desk. He was smiling at everything in the library, from the little table and chair by the window to the tiny maypops dotting the wallpaper. Scanning the bookshelves, he smiled even more. "I can still see her in here, curled up in the chair, nose in a book, lost in some adventure."

Lost in memory—that's what Cousin Richard was. Like I wasn't even in the room. "Never knew anybody to read more books than her."

"Aunt Tilley?"

He went solemn, shook his head. "Your mother."

I lowered my eyes.

He lifted my chin. "What do you say, let's not be sad right now. We'll have plenty of that tomorrow." Then he eyed the candy bag. "Can we split the last Hershey bar?" He was smiling again.

I said "Yes!" to Cousin Richard right there. And later, again and again in my head.

- - - - -

During all this time, Cousin Richard was one of the few people who didn't give me that awful pity look.

Pity looks from the townsfolk. Pity looks from kin.

And, oh, how I hated that awful waiting in most everybody's eyes. Like they were longing to see me cry.

Cousin Clare said as much. "No need to put up a brave front, my dear. Don't hold back. Let it out. Let it out," she whimpered, dabbing her eyes with a black hankie.

But I had no more tears.

I hadn't been able to stay strong the day Aunt Tilley died after all. That night, when I was in bed, I couldn't control myself. I had a big, long cry, with the sheet stuffed in my mouth for fear my sobs might carry down to The Traveler's Room and wake up Grandpa.

After that, though I missed Aunt Tilley so awful much, I never felt tears on the rise.

I didn't know how to tell Cousin Clare that I wasn't holding back from crying. I couldn't tell her much of anything. I certainly couldn't tell her how much I dreaded looking into her eyes.

Worse were the eyes I couldn't see.

Somebody staring at me.

Those mystery eyes were like red-hot burning coals.

I first felt them when we left the church. Felt them longest at the burial. During Revcrend

Curtis's final prayer, when all heads were bowed, I did a quick look around.

Just a scrawny peddler passing by. His slouch hat a little loose on his head.

- - - - -

"Amen."

After we tossed flowers on the coffin and the crowd began to ease away, Miss Ida handed me a basket with the silk flowers Grandpa had Adena's mother make. Then, Grandpa held my hand just as he had in church.

Made me remember times when I was little. How he rode me around the sitting room on his back. And the time I fell off the porch and got a big ole knot on my head, Grandpa had fussed over me so. Like I was all that mattered in the world.

I prayed Grandpa was going back to being gentle as just him and me stepped, hand in hand, over to four old graves. Each to get silk flowers.

Grandpa laid a ring of daisies on the first:

IN MEMORY OF LUCAS AND LUCINDA HANNIBAL
BELOVED SON AND DAUGHTER
OF SAMUEL AND DELIA HANNIBAL
DECEMBER 21, 1866–DECEMBER 24, 1866

Golden mums on the next:

IN MEMORY OF SAMUEL HANNIBAL, JR.
BELOVED SON
OF SAMUEL AND DELIA HANNIBAL
FEBRUARY 19, 1868–SEPTEMBER 18, 1887

For my grandma's grave, it was a red rose bouquet:

IN MEMORY OF DELIA HANNIBAL
BELOVED WIFE
OF SAMUEL HANNIBAL
FEBRUARY 15, 1841–JANUARY 17, 1888

And for my mother, purple maypops:

IN MEMORY OF JOLINE HANNIBAL
BELOVED DAUGHTER
OF SAMUEL AND DELIA HANNIBAL
APRIL 3, 1875–MARCH 7, 1893

- - - - -

I didn't feel those red-hot coals eyeing me again till we were back at the house. I was sitting on the red velvet settee between two old people. I'd picked that spot because I didn't have to deal with their eyes. They were closed.

On one side of me, Aunt Viney. On the other side, Uncle Matthias. She was praying, I believed. He, I knew, was asleep. His mouth was open.

That's when I felt Mystery Eyes again.

I looked to the front window, then to the side.

Nothing but daylight.

Then Aunt Viney whispered, "Somebody out back for you."

I knew better than to doubt Aunt Viney. I made haste—thinking at last I'd find out who was Mystery Eyes.

Five

Somebody was out back for me, but it wasn't Mystery Eyes. It was Adena with an apple stack cake.

"From our family to yours with sympathy," she said.

When I asked Adena to come in and have some punch—

"Can't," she said and smiled, then made her way down the back walk, her braids swinging in perfect rhythm with her wide-legged walk.

"Got more errands," Adena hollered over her shoulder, "then chores at home."

The first time I saw where home was for Adena was that day Viola got all vicious about her toes.

- - - - -

When Miss Tolliver dismissed us, Adena dashed away quick. Viola and a bunch of other kids followed fast, shouting "Lousy Lungin!"

Miss Tolliver looked so disgusted.

I was still in the classroom because it was my turn to be helper. I was about to wash the chalkboard when Miss Tolliver sighed. "Oh, dear, Adena left her satchel. Delana, would you do a good turn?"

I nodded.

I was always to go directly home after school, but I didn't know how to tell Miss Tolliver no. Besides, I owed Adena a kindness for even letting myself be tempted to do Viola's bidding.

Only problem, I didn't know where Adena lived.

When Miss Tolliver told me it was in the Hollow, I panicked. Aunt Tilley had told me the Hollow was full of people living a danger-life and ragamuffins running wild. But as I'd given my word, off I went, reminding myself to walk quick-quick and stay eagle-eyed.

As it turned out, I didn't see any wild and raggedy children in the Hollow. A few were barefoot, but none looked hungry. The danger-life people must've been asleep.

At Adena's house, the man out front fixing the porch railing didn't look dangerous at all. Just different. He was dark but not like me or any other colored person I'd ever seen. His hair was coal black and straight, like Cherokee or Chinese. His eyes were blue. Melungin, I guessed.

"Hello there." He smiled.

"Mr. Mullins?"

"Sure enough."

"I go to school with Adena. She left her things."

"Adena, my dear, you have a visitor!" he called into the house.

From the doorway, Adena looked to the left of me, then to the right before coming out to get her satchel.

"Thank you, Delana."

After "Welcome," I hurried on my way. Seconds later, I heard, "Delana, wait!"

I turned to see Adena running to me and also, her mama in the doorway, arms akimbo. Tall, big-boned Miss Lottie looked closer to colored than her husband. Like Adena.

And when Adena reached me, she took off her shoes, her socks. Gave me a full view of her feet, wriggling all her toes.

"You didn't have to prove anything to me, Adena."

After that, we started having bits of conversation during recess and after school let out. Adena became the closest thing I had to a friend.

On the day of Aunt Tilley's funeral, I so longed to have some conversation with Adena. None of the kinfolk brought any children. Some people from town had brought theirs, but "Hey" was the most any of them said to me. Even Viola Kimbrough. On her best behavior that day.

— — — — —

After I put the Mullins' apple stack cake on the kitchen table, I went upstairs and parked myself on the landing, in the spot where from below all a person looking up would see is shadow.

I sat still as stone, watching to see if anybody came out of the parlor or the sitting room or through the front door looking like they looking for me. I was hoping to spy Mystery Eyes. Maybe somebody had a miracle for me.

Didn't know I'd dozed off until the clock chimed.

As I came clear, it was to shuffling, rustling,

yawns, knuckle cracks, and other sounds grown-ups make when giving themselves a good, long stretch and loosening up their bones. Soon, the front and back screen doors were squeaking and slamming, squeaking and slamming. People were about to head out. By buggy. By train. Some by foot because home was near, and in Aunt Viney's case, because it was the way she lived.

After everybody left, where would that leave me?

When I moved to the top of the staircase, I saw the back of Aunt Viney. She was standing in the front door, tight grip on her doctor's bag. And calling me, it seemed, though she uttered not a word.

"Closer, chile," she said when I stopped at the bottom step. Not till I was by her side did Aunt Viney speak again. "Meek ain't weak, Delana. Meek ain't weak. Remember that."

I didn't know what else to say but, "Yes'm."

"And one more thing, dear girl. When God wish to bless, he sometime test. Remember that, too."

Aunt Viney pushed open the screen door, stepped out onto the porch, then down the stairs, only nodding her head to the left, to the right, but saying nothing to nobody as far as I could see.

When I stepped outside, I got good-bye hugs

and kisses from the women, pats on the shoulder from the men. To his pat, Cousin Richard added a fifty-cent piece.

So shiny. And brand-new: 1905. I could even read clear the word LIBERTY above the laurel wreath on the lady's head. Surely Cousin Richard had lots of fifty-cent pieces. He must've picked out the prettiest one for me.

"Thank you, Cousin Richard—and . . ."

"Yes, Delana?"

His glorious smile had me tongue-tied. There was so much I wanted to say, starting with, *Take me with you!*

If Cora had another boy and then couldn't have more children, but her and Cousin Richard had their hearts set on having a girl . . . maybe I would do. And one day they'd send Grandpa a telegram begging him to let me come live with them. Oh, how I wanted to tell Cousin Richard all of this. . . .

"Tell Cousin Cora, hey." That's all I could manage when my tongue got loose.

"Will do, Delana, will do."

I was about to ask Grandpa if I could ride with him to take Cousin Richard to the depot when he let me know I couldn't.

"Miss Nash will mind you till I get back."

As I stood on the porch, waving good-bye, I fiddled with my new fifty-cent piece. I was going to make a special keepsake pouch for it. Keep it in my nightstand drawer.

This coin was too special for the notions tin atop my wardrobe. That's where I kept the pennies, nickels, and other money gifts grownfolks had given me for earning high marks, for a Sunday school prize, or in a bag of Christmas candy I didn't get to eat much of.

Beside the notions tin was my wooden box of silver dollars. All from Grandpa. My birthday gifts. He'd count them out in my hand. One for each of my years.

"Save your money, Delana. Don't spend it on trifles. Save for something dear."

Same thing.

Same words.

Every year.

Like always, it was Aunt Tilley who'd filled in the gaps, helping me make sense of Grandpa's birthday gifts—why he said "save for something dear." She did it over time, the way she doled out candy.

At first, all I knew was that Grandpa had come up in slavery in Franklin County, Virginia—"With nothing to call his own—not even a claim on his own bones!" Aunt Tilley had said. By the time she died, I knew about the miracle way Grandpa got free.

How he learned a trade after his first master sold him to a colored man named Hannibal Watson with a posh barbershop for white gents. And how this Hannibal Watson let Grandpa keep his tips and take on all the side work he could scrounge up. Hannibal Watson, who treated Grandpa kind, had said he could buy himself for four hundred dollars.

So when Grandpa wasn't barbering he was keeping yards, hauling trash, chopping firewood, sweeping up saloons—in a powerful hurry-scurry to save up his freedom money. And when he had the whole four hundred dollars, Mr. Watson kept his word—with a miracle in the bargain.

Hannibal Watson told Grandpa that not four hundred, but just one dollar would do and urged him to make for Charleston. On top of that the man gave Grandpa names of folks here who could help him make a new life.

"Everlasting memento and reminder!" That was

Aunt Tilley on why Grandpa took the surname Hannibal.

The rabbit stew we had every first of August was a reminder meal. Rabbit stew was Hannibal Watson's favorite dish and the first of August, Grandpa's freedom day.

As for all his freedom money, that was seed, Aunt Tilley had said, for the barbershops for white gents he now had and the houses he rented out to colored and white.

What I didn't know was if Grandpa wanted me to have shops and property when I grew up. Or was it that he feared the Ku Kluxers would come to rule the nation and bring slavery back? Then I'd need some freedom money stashed away.

I never asked Aunt Tilley about that or how she got free. I always figured she'd tell me by and by. And I was used to waiting.

- - - - -

Waiting. For I knew not what. Waiting. For some miracle in my life like Grandpa got.

Everybody was long gone but there I was still on the porch. Waiting. I dreaded going inside, dreaded the quiet I'd find.

Never much of that when Aunt Tilley was alive. Always talking. Telling me what to do, how to be. If not that, telling me stories.

And there had been all her talk about what to beware, like boys with Cheshire cat smiles, boys who say they want to show me a bunny in a barn, boys who set off firecrackers, boys who go *Psst!* from behind a bush, white trash, colored trash, people who pray loud, people who don't pray at all, lazy fools, fairs, Circus Day, ripping and running, jack-leg preachers, pawnbrokers, pistols, women who gussy up, floozies, men with a wily eye, Melungins, the Hollow, people who beg for bones, boys who act grown. And Jude.

Jude did errands and odd jobs at Grandpa's shop in the Ruffner Hotel and at our house sometimes. Jude was tall, rail thin, and had big puppy-dog eyes. About fifteen and on his own, but he didn't look to me like he lived a danger-life. I couldn't understand why Aunt Tilley put him on the list of bewares.

The stove was on the temporary list of what to beware like most else in the kitchen. All I ever got to do was stir lemonade, string and snap beans, beat batter. Watch sweet tea cool.

No real cooking lest I catch on fire. No chopping, slicing, peeling—nothing with a knife lest I cut myself and bleed to death. I couldn't work the grinder because I'd end up with chewed-up fingers.

My day would come, Aunt Tilley always promised. Till then, real cooking was on the list of bewares.

She had even given me a tablet—

"Write down all my cautions!"

Across the top of the tablet, she had me write "The Book of Bewares."

The night before she died, Aunt Tilley had me add saloons and Wheeling, West Virginia, to *The Book of Bewares.*

I'd long ago put dragonflies in the book. And dragonfly dreams. Aunt Tilley had said my nightmare was Father God's way of telling me "there's something to beware."

When Aunt Tilley wasn't telling me what to beware, on occasion she gave me alerts about things up ahead. For my thirteenth birthday, I'd be getting my picture taken at Gates. She told me that on the day we were visiting some of Uncle Dub's people when they were young. People I hoped to meet one day given how exciting their lives seemed.

There was the tintype of Uncle Dub's little sister, Victoria, who looked like she didn't want to be in that chair and who grew up to be a woman who stayed on the move. Aunt Tilley had said Victoria became one of our best lady reporters, writing for the *Washington Bee*, the *Women's Era*, and a heap more newspapers and magazines.

And there was the cabinet card of another sister's children—Peter, Peonia, and Penelope. All three still living in Missouri and running the family's pharmacy that had a soda fountain up front. As I tried to imagine what they looked like grown, I asked Aunt Tilley why there were no pictures of me.

"Your day will come," she said softly, looking like she was roaming around in her head. "Your day will come." She even seemed a touch sad. "When you turn thirteen, Delana, you'll be getting your picture taken at Gates . . . when you turn thirteen."

"Why thirteen?"

Aunt Tilley came alert. "Thirteen, well, um, that's the age of accountability."

"What happens then?"

"Your sins start to count." Without another word, Aunt Tilley rushed from the parlor.

- - - - -

As I stood on the porch dreading the quiet, I feared that with Aunt Tilley gone, I'd never get my picture taken. I had four whole months to wait. And hope. Could be she told Grandpa or Miss Ida about her plans. Maybe one of them would take me to Gates.

I also had four months to sin at no cost, I realized. Only one wickedness had ever crossed my mind. Slapping Viola Kimbrough. When she kicked me. When she tripped me. When she called me "Dumb Delana" in a stabbing or ghosty voice.

The screen door squeaked.

It was Miss Ida. "Getting too chilly to be outdoors."

Inside, she looked at me hard, told me I looked a bit peaked. I didn't feel sick, but she sure was fidgety. Shifting from foot to foot. Wringing her hands. She must've feared Grandpa would be angry with her if I came down sick. "Best go upstairs and rest yourself awhile," she cooed. "Hurry now, hurry."

I headed upstairs to do as I was told, but when I entered my room, I nearabout jumped out my skin.

A small yalla hand clamped over my mouth. A boot kicked the door close.

I saw fire in the eyes, but not the Devil.

Six

D on't be scared."

The voice was a whisper. The face familiar.

I was more flabbergasted than scared.

"Swear you won't cry out?"

I nodded as best I could.

As the hand lifted from over my mouth, again came a whisper. "I'm your cousin—"

"Ambertine?" I whispered back.

The fire in her eyes dimmed. She grinned.

Ambertine didn't look all that much older, but she was bonier than in her picture. And so tiny. Shorter than me. Not all gussied up either—no beehive-busy black dress, no Ali Baba hat. Nothing like that. She was done up like a man!

Beat-up boots.

Denim trousers.

Checked shirt.

Ratty corduroy sack coat.

And on her head—

That's when it hit me.

A slouch hat—a little loose on her head.

"At the burial—you passed by," I gasped, took a step back. Right then and there I knew! Ambertine was Mystery Eyes!

And she hugged me, hugged me hard, like she knew I wouldn't break. "Delana," she said with a sigh, rocking me, as she repeated my name over and over again. "Sorry for the startle, but there was no other way. I'm not welcome here."

When she let me go, her eyes were glistening.

I was still stunned.

"'Trash and trouble'!" Ambertine whisper-hissed, easing down on the chest at the foot of my bed. "'Sold her soul to the Devil' . . . That's some of what you heard said of me, ain't it?"

I felt bad for her. And puzzled. How did she know what Aunt Tilley said?

But from the looks of her, Ambertine didn't seem fazed. "Been called worse, a lot worse," she said. "Truth is, I ain't no pretty Christian picture. Cuss. Swig liquor. The soul that crosses me might get cut. And my money comes rough—off other people's miseries. Pawnbroker."

I could hear Aunt Tilley—*loud!*

Beware!

Beware!

Beware!

Amberline leaned in. "If you fear me, I will leave. If not, hear me out, Delana, and with the knowing part of your soul."

I couldn't take my eyes off hers, with their flecks of gold and a yonder gaze. Like Aunt Viney.

"Your choice," Ambertine whispered.

"Stay."

It came out easy, like Ambertine being there was the most normal thing in the world. I felt safe. Aunt Tilley's *Beware! Beware! Beware!* was like a fading echo in a forest far away.

Then came another shock.

"I wager you was never told that me and your mama were like sisters."

I shook my head. "Never."

"Joline never judged me . . . Joline wept heavy for me when she seen me bruised and welted up from Pa beating on me because I skipped school or gave him a queer look and some sass."

Ambertine was over by my bureau, gazing out the window that opened onto an elm tree. "Night I lit out for Chicago with a flashy young fella passing through town, I said good-bye to your mama from a tree like this one that used to be outside her window."

There was no tree outside any other window, but beneath the room with sandy white furniture, there was a tree stump.

"Two rooms down . . . that was my mother's?"

Ambertine nodded. "And on the night I left, when she came to her window, we whispered quick. Me telling her to watch for word from Bertha Mason."

Aunt Tilley had never made mention of anybody by that name. "Bertha Mason? Another cousin?" I asked Ambertine.

"No, sugar, she's a character from *Jane Eyre*. Story about a governess living in spooky Thornfield Manor. Of all the books Joline and I started reading together, *Jane Eyre* was the only one I seen through. Your mama had most sympathy for Jane, what with her being an orphan and all, and soft. I felt more sorry for crazy Bertha Mason. Wife of Jane's boss man, nasty Mr. Rochester."

The way she spat out his name, I believed if Ambertine was in that story she would've cut that man or went swinging and swacking at him with an umbrella.

"Anyways," she continued, "after I left Charleston, not a week passed that your mama and me didn't write. She was always ready with a story about making friends with an out-of-towner at a tea or church function, should anybody ask about her letters to and from Miss Bertha Mason."

From her coat pocket, Ambertine brought out an envelope and handed it to me. "The last letter I got from your mama. The shortest one, too."

It was addressed, in a beautiful cursive, to Miss Bertha Mason. Not in Chicago. In Kansas City.

Ambertine read my mind. "I move around," she said, looking at the envelope, then back at me. "Go on, open it."

It *was* short. Just six words.

Keep watch over my baby girl.

J.

My bottom lip trembled as I read the note again, noticing the drawing of purple maypops up top.

"That's what I've been doing, Delana. Keeping watch."

How? I wondered. *From Chicago? From Kansas City? From—?* This didn't make sense. I no longer felt safe.

"I'm resourceful, my dear Delana." Ambertine rose, moved toward me, her eyes going narrow like she could see into my very soul. "Your favorite subject? Would that be geography?"

I nodded.

Aunt Tilley's voice was back in my head, telling me, *Beware!*

"Just this year your womanhood came on. Am I right?" Ambertine next asked, taking another step.

"What Aunt Tilley called the curse?"

Ambertine rolled her eyes. "Right.... And there's something else I know I'm right about, Delana. This locked-up life ain't what your mama would want for you.... Second of March you'll be thirteen, right?"

"Yes'm."

"What do you want, Delana?"

Nobody had ever asked me that. Not about my birthday or Christmas or anything else.

"What do you want, Delana?" Ambertine asked again.

I said the first thing that popped in my head. "A globe."

Ambertine frowned, rolled her eyes again. "No, sugar, not for your birthday. What do you want for your life. Ain't you never daydreamed about your future?"

"Not really."

"Never seen a dress in a store window on Capitol Street or in the Sears or Marshall catalog that you fancied your grown self wearing one day?"

"Always figured Aunt Tilley would tell me what was to be in my future. . . . I'm not fixed to want big things."

"Sure you are. Everybody's fixed to dream, till something or somebody break their spirit." Ambertine looked like a judge laying down a law. "Your life don't have to be based on what Aunt Tilley said. When I got word she was gone, I decided it was time for you to know some things, get some freedom wings. What do you say? What do you want?"

I started to say I wanted to see Aunt Tilley's wishing-place and to live with Cousin Richard, but I was too scrambled to speak. One minute

Ambertine seemed safe. The next, like she belonged in *The Book of Bewares*.

I looked at my mother's note, then back at Ambertine. She was over at my dresser, picking through the basket of kinfolk.

Ambertine smiled a time or two, grunted some. Paused only once. When she had the picture of herself in her hand. "Sent this to my folks from Chicago," she muttered. "To let them know I was still among the living. Never heard back."

Ambertine looked like a little girl, but as soon as she went back to rooting through the photographs she was fiery again.

"Not one of your mama?"

I shook my head. "Nor of Grandma Delia, Lucas and Lucinda, or Junior. Aunt Tilley said their pictures, along with ones of my mother...Grandpa buried all them with her. Wanted her to have some of family in Heaven."

I told Ambertine Aunt Tilley rarely spoke about my mother other than to say that she was an angel. "Said best I don't bring her up around Grandpa, for that would bring on a storm of sorrowful memories more than he can bear. Might kill him. Visits to the graves were hard enough on him, Aunt Tilley said."

Ambertine sucked her teeth. "Come over here."

When I reached her, Ambertine held my head between her hands. She had me look straight into the mirror above my dresser.

"When you see yourself, you see your mama."

I stared at myself, then at Ambertine's reflection eyeballing me, then back at myself.

Could this be why Grandpa didn't put much time into me—I brought on a storm of sorrowful memories? Maybe he didn't hate me.

"Your mama had spirit, Delana. She had fire," Ambertine said softly, making me wonder if I had some hidden spirit, a secret fire.

"Joline could dream big and far and wide. Like if she saw in a catalog or shop window a glorious dress, she pictured herself in it. In a flash, she was conjuring a story about being up in New York City or across the ocean in Paris, France, strolling down a boulevard in that glorious dress, and with a glamorous hat and parasol to match. Head held high."

Ambertine struck a fancy-lady pose. Like Eula. Top boss of her world.

"Same with a painting—be it mountains, forest, a seaside, it made no matter, Joline put herself in the scene. She dreamed herself a world." Ambertine threw her head back and spread her arms out wide. "Joline liked what she liked—didn't make no never mind what otherbodies thought. And Lord knows, she could take a liking to the most peculiar things. Purple maypops, I could understand. But box turtles? Oyster shells? And nothing topped her fancy for fish scales."

"Fish scales?" I frowned, recollecting times I watched Miss Ida out back clean walleye or other fish, their scales flicking and flying all over the place.

"Not what you thinking." Ambertine chuckled. "I'm talking about a coin, a three-cent silver piece. Tiny like some fish scales. Those little coins used to turn up in the back of drawers, linings, cracks in floorboards. So small I reckon more lost than spent. Your mama adored those little things. Where others saw scrap, Joline saw moons, stars—the whole of Heaven." Ambertine was wonderlit.

And we were face-to-face. Ambertine had me by the shoulders. "Then came the day," she said, "when your mama met a man who became her world."

She was mind reading again. "Yes, Delana, your father, Jordan Burkett."

Aunt Tilley said his name was Lucifer and that he'd been too lazy to carry a surname.

"Your mama loved him so. And he loved her."

Jordan Burkett.

I said his name over and over again in my head. Fighting back tears, I told Ambertine the story I'd been raised on.

That my father only took up with my mother because he saw this big house, knew about Grandpa having property and barbershops, but then he ran off for better pickings. "Right before I was born," I sniffled. "Aunt Tilley said my mother used her last bit of strength to bring me into the world."

The story sounded worse—hurt worse—coming from my mouth. When Aunt Tilley told it, she was hugging me, and saying that in the end all was right with the world because I was now with her, safe and sound, and my mother was up in Heaven doing angel work.

"Aunt Tilley lied, Delana." Ambertine didn't sound cruel, but like she really did have a hiding kindness.

Ambertine, my room, everything—a blur. As I cried, Ambertine hugged me, rocked me, but I didn't feel safe and sound. I felt confused. Scared. Upside down.

"Truth, Delana. Him for her, her for him. Your folks had a powerful love both ways."

I still couldn't believe what I was hearing. "You saying my father wasn't just a no-good—"

"Your father is not no-good!"

"Then why'd he run off?"

"He didn't run off! He faced a hard choice."

Stair steps creaked.

We both flinched.

Ambertine put a pointer finger to her lips, then jumped, jackrabbit, into my wardrobe. And a pistol hit the floor.

I jumped. Not into the wardrobe but back up against my bed. Then, more panicky over the footsteps coming down the hall than over the pistol, I kicked it under my bed. Next, I slipped the envelope under my pillow.

I knew by the knock who was there.

"Yes, Grandpa." I wiped my face.

"You decent?"

"Yessir." I opened the door.

Grandpa bit his lip, frowned. "You all right?"

I nodded. "Don't worry, Grandpa, I'm being strong."

"Well, that's good. . . . And for now, I need for you to come say good night to Miss Ida."

I followed him down the back stairs and into the kitchen, where Miss Ida was packing up dishes and pans of hers.

"Thank you, Miss Ida, for everything."

She patted my cheek. "You more than welcome."

Grandpa grabbed the heaviest pile of pots. "Going to help Miss Ida home. Won't be long."

I hoped otherwise. Maybe she'd invite Grandpa in for pie or coffee.

As soon as those two were down the back porch stairs, I hurried up to my room.

Do you have a picture of my mother?

Of my father?

And did I hear you right?—"Your father is not no-good!"

He's still alive?

Aunt Tilley said he was dead.

I couldn't get up to my room fast enough.

When I did, my window was wide open. My curtains, giving salutes.

I checked my wardrobe. No Ambertine.

I looked under my bed. No pistol.

The envelope was still under my pillow. I read the note again.

Keep watch over my baby girl.

As I closed my window, I saw something new about the elm tree. Bare as it was, with just a few leaves waving back at the breeze, what I saw was a sturdy black hand surging up from the earth, ready to be a rescue.

Then a little silver something on my bureau caught my eye. Only when I had the coin in my hand did I delight at the stars, did I smile at the moons.

I wanted to dream myself a world.

Seven

"Your mother was an angel. Make her proud."
That was the message on the postcard from Cousin Clare.

I had made lots of visits to that funeral guest book so I could write kinfolk. Telling them how good it was to meet even if the occasion was sorrowful. Telling them I thought maybe they would like to know some things about me, like my favorite color (yellow), favorite flower (yellow-faced pansies), and how well I do at needlework.

After I figured I'd done enough polite talk, I got down to what I really cared about. Asking for memories of my folks.

Most of my letters took up two sheets.

Owego, N. Y.

MARKET ST. PARKERSBURG, W. VA.

Postcards. That's all I got back.

Could have been worse. Nobody could have written back at all. And this was the first time I'd gotten any kind of mail in my whole life. Postcards were better than nothing.

Cousin Clare's was of Market Street in Parkersburg.

Make her proud.

Her message was a little something to latch on to. I'd make my mother proud by doing like Ambertine said she did. I put myself in the scene.

I pictured myself walking down Market Street, looking in all the shop windows. When I saw something I liked, I walked right in the store—head held high—and I bought it, no matter what otherbodies thought. Only thing was I couldn't imagine what "it" was.

The postcard from Uncle Matthias was a wonder. It wasn't of somewhere in Madison, but in Owego, New York.

I reckoned he'd collected thousands of postcards from all the cities his railroad job took him to. The scene from Owego was of railroad track by a riverbank and facing a mountain bend up ahead.

I put myself in this scene, too.

I imagined myself on a train traveling that track. Suddenly, I was holding my breath for fear the train was going too fast—might not slow in time to take the curve. And if we made it safe to the other side, what would I see? A village? A valley? More mountains?

An abyss? Like Reverend Curtis preached about a few weeks back? A place for the Devil and his demons. A blacker-than-midnight bottomless pit.

"Hope you enjoy this scene." That's what Uncle Matthias scrawled.

I had liked the scene. Until I put myself in it, that is. Besides, I wanted more than a scene from Uncle Matthias. I wanted *information and news.* Along with memories of my folks, I'd asked him where Ambertine lives. I explained how I knew she was kin and maybe she didn't know Aunt Tilley had gone to be with the Lord. Given he used to be a human telegraph, I figured if Uncle Matthias didn't know where Ambertine was, he could find out.

- - - - -

"Write him again."

That was Adena. School had just let out. On other days, I'd told her all about Aunt Tilley's funeral and everything about Ambertine's secret visit. I had even let Adena see my mother's note. The three-cent silver, too.

"When I go to sleep, they're under my mattress. When I'm awake, on me." I showed her how I slip-stitched pockets on the underside of my skirts and dresses.

I knew Adena wouldn't tell a soul and that she'd also help me think, but her idea about writing Uncle Matthias a second time didn't sit well. "He might think me impudent—and I don't want him casting no wily eye on me. Not even from a distance."

"Then just wait. You said Ambertine seemed like one on a mission. I say she's not done with you. If she been watching over you all these years, don't make sense for her to stop now."

Adena sounded so sure. And maybe she was right. Ambertine wasn't done with me. But where was she now? "I don't want to wait, Adena. I have to find Ambertine—I have to know if my pa is alive and about the hard choice she said he faced. Why he left me."

There was something else.

"I also want to know if Ambertine is . . . well,

maybe she can watch over me and come and go by windows because—"

I came to a standstill and looked at Adena.

She stopped walking, too, and looked at me.

"Adena, what if Ambertine is a witch?"

"Why would a witch need a pistol?" Adena frowned. "Could be like with your aunt Viney. That the Holy Spirit speaks to Ambertine."

"But Ambertine's a sinner."

"That don't mean God didn't give her gifts."

Then Adena asked about Cousin Richard.

"Like everybody else . . . a postcard," I told her. "Some Pennsylvania pastureland with cows, chewing the cud, I suppose. 'Thinking of you,' he wrote. Might could be he already gave me his best memory of my mother, about how she loved books. And maybe he never knew my father. Or . . ."

That telegram asking me to be their daughter would never arrive, I feared. Cousin Richard wouldn't be coming to get me. We'd never sit side by side on a train to Pennsylvania. I'd never set foot in their house and say to Cousin Cora, "Hello, it's so nice to meet you," and have her smile and say, "Oh, Delana, you are my child of promise! You must call me Ma!" Then Cousin Richard would say, "And you must call me Pa!" They'd hug me hard and tell me I was mighty dear to them.

I didn't say all that to Adena, only "Could be Cousin Richard done left me, too."

Adena didn't think so. "Could be the baby came the same day as your letter and he's running around like a chicken with his head cut off. He's got to be plenty worn with one life leaving him and another coming."

Maybe, I thought. And anyways, if my father was still alive he was the one I wanted to call Pa.

A few seconds later, Adena added, "You know who could tell you how to find Ambertine—and maybe your pa, too?"

"I know. Aunt Viney. But all she wrote in the guest book was her name. But I've prayed, Adena. I asked the Holy Spirit to tap Aunt Viney on the shoulder wherever she is, spirit-speak to her—tell her to tilt back to me."

Adena stopped and looked at me. "Why not ask your grandpa about your pa?"

"I can't do that! Aunt Tilley said I must *never* bring him up, especially not to Grandpa."

"Any harm bringing up Ambertine? Can't you just ask him where she stay? Say to him what you told your uncle Matthias. Don't let on you know more about her than he thinks you know."

Adena made good sense now. When she went her way and I mine, I started summoning up the courage to ask Grandpa about Ambertine.

Eight

Miss Ida wasn't in the kitchen.

Not in the dining room.

I checked the sitting room. Next, the parlor.

I hollered up the stairs. "Miss Ida!"

Strange. She was always there when I came home.

There were times I ached all over to ask Grandpa if Miss Ida could live with us—tell him how awful nights were for me. Upstairs all by myself. Worse, after that dragonfly nightmare came back.

Sewing up my lids.

Stitching shut my lips.

When I told Miss Ida about the dream, she said it was just something I ate kicking up a ruckus. Dragonflies were nothing to fear, she insisted.

"They are one of God's joys to the world. Sign of a better day coming! Of new beginnings!"

"Miss Ida!" I hollered up the stairs again, then went back into the sitting room, through the dining room, and into the kitchen.

"Grandpa?"

I tiptoed past the pantry to The Traveler's Room. Maybe he was taking a nap.

I knocked.

No answer.

I eased the door open.

No Grandpa.

I ran a finger over the door's plaque that read "The Traveler's Room," recalling the day I asked Aunt Tilley about Grandpa's room.

Just her and me in the kitchen. She doing up shuck beans. Me watching.

I had just learned to read.

"Grandpa's real name The Traveler?"

"No, baby." Aunt Tilley laughed. "It's Sam, like you always hear me call him. Short for Samuel." She then told me how The Traveler's Room came to be.

"A long, long time ago, long before you were born, when Sam was making his way to Charleston, sleeping in the woods, or in a barn if a farmer was kind . . ." Aunt Tilley's eyes went wide. "Well, one night when the rain was a-lashin' and the wind was a-whippin'—Lawdamercy, what a wretched, wretched night! And your grandpa so bone-weary when he knocked on the door of a farmhouse down around New River. He asked the Mister could he take a rest in his barn. And guess what?"

"What?" I was wide-eyed, too.

"Glory to Father God! It was a house where mercy abounded! Mercy abounded!"

Aunt Tilley cleared her throat, getting ready to playact.

"Traveler." Her voice was deep. "Traveler, I wouldn't let a dog sleep in the barn on such a night as this." In her own voice, Aunt Tilley continued. "That's what the man of the house said when he invited your grandpa in. Then the Mister and the Missus give your grandpa a change of clothes so his could dry by the fire, warmed his insides with a big bowl of soup. Time come to turn in, they led him to a little room off the pantry. Simple room— narrow iron bed, pine chest of drawers, pine wardrobe, cane chair. Best sleep he'd had in days. Next morning, he lit out early, not wanting to wear out his welcome. Left a silver dollar on the bed."

Aunt Tilley soon had on her whisper voice. "That good night's sleep wasn't the end of the blessing, oh, no! After Sam got hisself settled here in Charleston, he went back to that house where mercy abounded. Wanted to thank that kind couple, proper, with a tin of fancy tea. When he did, he met the sons and daughters he'd not seen on that nasty night. One daughter caught his eye. Can you guess her name?"

"The Traveler?" I replied in my whisper-voice.

"No, no, no! Her name was Delia!"

"Grandma in Heaven?" I beamed.

"That's right!" Pointing to The Traveler's Room, Aunt Tilley then explained that when Grandpa was building this house, he had planned for a small room behind the pantry. "Had one of the carpenters make that plaque. Furnished the room just like his room of refuge, ready should wretched weather bring a stranger to his door."

Years later, when I asked why Grandpa slept in The Traveler's Room instead of in a bedroom upstairs with fine furniture, Aunt Tilley told me to add "a curious cat" to *The Book of Bewares*.

Now, as I made my way up the back stairs, I wondered if Aunt Tilley's story about The Traveler's

Room and every other story she told me was true. If she had lied about my ma and pa—

I froze when I saw an envelope on my pillow.

"Delana" was the only thing written on the envelope. Inside it, wrapped up in a letter, was a tintype.

Three pretty ladies.

The one standing on the left looked sassy. The one on the right, serene. Seated between them, looking so strong, staring straight at me—

Dear Delana,

Your mama had this picture taken years ago when she was up in Wheeling for the yearly Tri-State Emancipation Celebration. She called it her first "on my own." She'd never been out of Charleston.

To the left of her is Bethany Rice. To the right is Bethany's sister, Miriam. Summer before, they come from Wheeling to Charleston to visit an uncle. Your mama met them at a tea. Hit it off right away. They begged her to come visit them during the freedom festivities coming up that September.

The Rice girls told your mama of the glorious time she was sure to have at the parade, at the fair. There'd be a ball, too. They also told her some of their Charleston kin was coming so she'd have company for the journey.

Up in Wheeling, that's where Joline met Jordan.

"He's so full of life!" That's what your mama wrote me about him. Said he was living, breathing adventure. Had mined silver in Nevada, outrun alligators when draining swampland down in the Everglades, and sailed the seas on fishing ships out of Nova Scotia. Your pa had recently come to Wheeling. He and some cousins were cooking up an enterprise.

"I am going to marry this man! I am going to have a vivid life!" That's what your mama wrote me.

Decide what you want, Delana.

Watching Over You,
A.

Now it was my own hand clamped over my mouth lest all of Kanawha County hear my cries.

I buried my face in my pillow to muffle myself more. When the tears let up, I looked at my mother again, read Ambertine's letter again, cried again.

I felt a heap of hate for Aunt Tilley—for all the lies!

No boys with Cheshire cat smiles!

No jackleg preachers!

No people who beg for bones!

I couldn't imagine nobody—*nothing*—doing me more harm, being more a danger than Aunt Tilley. All along, she was the biggest *Beware!* All her lies!

In my nightstand drawer was *The Book of Bewares*. I could hear Aunt Tilley crying out from the grave, *You gonna need my cautions!*

I didn't care.

I tore up *The Book of Bewares*.

And Grandpa? Why didn't he ever tell Aunt Tilley to hush and tell me the truth? I hated them both. I was going to hate them forever and didn't care that this sin would count soon.

I looked at the picture again, dabbed away the teardrops with my cuff.

"Mama . . ."

First time in my life I ever said that word.

"Mama . . ."

I wanted to believe she could hear me . . . wanted to believe she was seeing me meet her likeness and knowing she loved my father and three-cent silver.

Suddenly, I felt the strength of a second self.

When I heard noises downstairs, calmly I put the letter and the tintype back in the envelope, then slipped it in the pocket with my mother's note and the three-cent silver. Next, I fastened my cloak, walked over to my window, and looked down at the sturdy black hand surging up from the earth.

I took a deep breath and trusted the knowing part of my soul—climbed down that tree like I'd done it a hundred times before, then ran to the only place I could think to go.

To the Hollow.

Nine

S he out back."

That was Adena's little brother, Micah.

"Adena!" he hollered as he dashed back into the house. "Sad girl here to see you!"

I plopped down on the top step. Dazed.

"What happened?" gasped Adena, joining me. "You look like you seen a ghost."

With the dark patches on her face and hands, Adena looked like she had been dumping coal ash.

"Adena, you were right about Ambertine." I held up the envelope. "From her. Not only is she not done with me, she's close by. Just my name. No stamp. No postmark. And you won't believe what's inside."

I handed Adena the envelope. She wiped her hands on her apron, but there was no rubbing all the soot away. "Better you show me," she said.

The photograph first. "The one in the middle."

"Your mama?"

I nodded.

"She's pretty."

Suddenly, I was all choked up. I thought my mother was pretty the minute I looked at her, but then remembered that Ambertine said I looked like my mother. I'd never felt pretty in my life.

A nice girl. A good girl—those were the kinds of things grownfolks said about me. Never that I was pretty. And when Viola wasn't calling me dumb, she was oftentimes snickering "Blackie" or hissing "Ugly Bug" at me.

"Thank you," I said to Adena, still fighting back tears. Then I put Ambertine's letter up to her eyes.

It didn't take Adena long to read it through. I was much better at memory things like Bible verses and poems. She was the faster reader.

"Your pa don't sound like a bad man at all, Delana. And your ma . . . she's got a power to her. Can't see a man running off from her. And, you know, their names, Joline and Jordan, they match up nice . . . like how our names could be sisters." Adena was trying hard to cheer me up.

It was working.

A little.

I still felt dazed. And weak. That stronger second self that got me out my window, down my tree, and to the Hollow was playing hide-and-go-seek on me.

Just like Ambertine.

Why?

I was starting to think Ambertine didn't have a hiding kindness at all. More like she was cruel. Or maybe came down with an early case of whatever made Aunt Tilley get so twitchy.

Why didn't Ambertine just lay everything out for me, like Aunt Tilley and now Miss Ida laid out my clothes. What did Ambertine want me to decide—and want me to want?

"You decide what you want?" Adena asked, her mind tracking mine.

"To know why Ambertine's doing this to me, acting like a shadow. Why don't she just come out and tell me all she knows and if my father—"

I looked at my mother again. Adena was right, she did have a power to her. I could sense her spirit, her fire, and I wanted more.

"Adena, you ever lost somebody?"

She nodded. "Grandma on Pa's side, when we lived in Tennessee. In Kentucky, I had a big brother, Sherman. A rusty nail made his foot rotten, then the rest of him."

"How well you remember your brother?"

"Get whiffs sometimes. See a picture in my mind of a tall boy walking me, feeding me. First time I told Mama about it, she said it was Sherman all right." Adena sighed. "Sometimes when I'm out in the woods picking berries . . . I hear a voice say to me, 'Watch your step.' Sure enough some critter scampers out from where I was about to walk . . . and I know Sherman was being my watchout."

"And your grandma?"

"She comes to me all the time. Like when I'm kneading dough and my hands get tired and I'm ready to quit. Then I hear my grandma saying, 'Thorough, Adena, do it thorough.' And I keep kneading with a new strength."

"Aunt Tilley came to me plenty after she died, but I don't want her near me no more."

"You might not have a say in that."

"Why not?"

"I don't think the living call up the dead, Delana. I think the dead summon themselves up into our lives."

Why had my mother never come to me?

"Your brother Sherman loved you, right?"

Adena nodded.

"And your grandma?"

She nodded something fierce.

"Never even had a whiff of my mother, Adena. Think that means she didn't love—"

"Oh no, Delana, don't think that! Your mama loved you! She never would've told Ambertine to watch over you if she didn't love you."

That made me feel a little better. It felt true. And yet, Adena looked puzzled, strange.

"What's wrong now?"

"Nothing."

"Tell me, Adena."

"You won't like it."

"Go on anyway. I'm getting used to pain."

"It's not something I know for sure, Delana. Something I only wonder."

"Say it."

"Can the dead come to us if we don't remember them?" Adena fiddled with her laces. "What if our memories are like a drawbridge let down between our world and the next."

Adena was right. I didn't like what she had to

say. Having no memory of my mother was bad enough. The notion that she would never ever come to me because I had no memories of her—

Unless—

"Adena, you think the dead can cross over on secondhand memories?"

She shrugged. "Possible."

We sat silent for a while, watching a cat with a caravan of kittens tramp into the field across the road.

Soon, Adena and I were back to talking about the dead.

"Minute Aunt Tilley reached Heaven, I reckon my mother went at her madder than a wet hen for telling me all those lies."

"Can't fuss and fight in Heaven."

"So long as you don't do bodily harm, can't you say your piece?"

One kitten was scrambling from the field, out to the road. The mother cat was soon there, grabbing her baby by the scruff for toting back into the tall mass of weeds.

Adena and I switched up to what we'd do when we were dead. All I could think about was talking to my mother. Dawn to dusk. Dusk to dark. Adena looked forward to seeing Sherman all healed and eating her grandma's butter rolls.

That willful kitten was near to the road again. Like before, the mama wasn't far behind.

And Adena had something else for dead us to do. "Come nightfall, we swoop down and haunt Viola Kimbrough!" I'd never seen Adena smile so. I smiled, too.

I was back to wondering if the dead can cross over on secondhand—or maybe make-believe—memories when Adena shot up and raced to the road.

Her mama was coming home.

- - - - -

Miss Lottie had a sack over one shoulder and an empty basket on one hip. She was all lace and lavender as Adena took the sack from her, but when Miss Lottie saw me, she turned sour. She started walking faster toward me, like a fright, her black cape flapping like a raven's wings.

Adena skipped to keep up.

"Delana! Your grandpa done sounded the alarm, got folks searching for you!" Miss Lottie dropped the basket on the ground. She towered over me, arms akimbo, like Goliath before David. "Ida Nash about to lose her mind. I was at the Kimbrough place when she come there asking if anybody seen you since school let out, babbling about how she lost track of time on errands."

I looked to Adena for rescue.

"I was feeling poorly after school. She helped me home," Adena said.

Miss Lottie harrumphed, grabbed me by the arm, and marched me up the road. I tried to tell her she didn't have to put herself out. I promised to go straight home.

"Most surely, but not without me, missy. Something happen to you between here and home, there'll be no living it down when folks find out you was last seen at my place."

Miss Lottie had us walking faster and faster the closer we got to my home. And my heart, it thump-thumped louder.

And louder.

Lawdamercy, what would Grandpa do to me?

- - - - -

When we turned onto Shrewsbury, I saw someone sitting on the front steps.

It was Jude. With the puppy-dog eyes.

As soon as Jude spotted us, he jumped up and hollered at the house, "She found, Mr. Hannibal! She found!"

Before Miss Lottie and I reached the walkway, Grandpa was through the front door.

High boots.

Denim jacket.

His traveling hat in his hand.

Grandpa was dressed like he does when he goes for a day or overnight to check on a property or barbershop.

All he did was stare at me.

Miss Lottie, huffing and puffing, commenced talking like the hangman was near.

"Mr. Hannibal, when I come home from deliveries, what do I find but your Delana. Seems my Adena was feeling poorly when school let out. Delana seen her home. I swear Mr.—"

Grandpa raised his pointer finger. Miss Lottie hushed. "I got no quarrel with you and your'n, Mrs. Mullins. I thank you for bringing Delana home."

Grandpa looked calm but there was something brewing in his voice. And he was fiddling with his pocket change.

Next, I heard footsteps behind me, then "Thank you, Jesus!"

Miss Ida.

Grandpa came to the top step. "All's well now. Y'all can go home now." He flipped Jude a piece of change.

Jude caught the coin in one smooth move. "Thank you, sir, Mr. Hannibal," he said, tipping his hat. Then Jude skittled down the steps and was in the wind.

Next, Miss Lottie took her leave. "Good day, Mr. Hannibal," she said with a nod.

Miss Ida headed to the back of the house. "Supper be on the table in a few minutes."

Grandpa stopped her with two words: "No need."

Not until Miss Ida was far along on her way home did Grandpa speak again.

"Quite a scare you give me. All sorts of things run through my mind."

"Sorry, Grandpa," I said to the ground.

"Look at me when I speak to you!"

He had never yelled at me before.

I looked up. "Yessir, I'm sorry, sir."

"Next time something like that happens, don't linger!" he snapped, then opened the screen door.

I couldn't move. The thought of being in that house, just me and him—

"Don't try me, Delana," Grandpa said over his shoulder. "Git in the house!"

When I still didn't move, he spun around all angry-eyed.

I flinched, stepped back.

He had never struck me, yet I feared a beating like Ambertine got from her pa. But if anybody had a right to be riled, it was *me*. I was the one lied to and all jumbled up.

Then I heard Aunt Viney.

Meek ain't weak, Delana. Meek ain't weak.

"Adena didn't take sick," I blurted out. That strength of a second self that got me down my elm tree was back. "I came right home after school, Grandpa. Then I left—left by the tree outside my window—because of this."

Ten

Tears were streaming down my face.

In my outstretched hand was the envelope with my mother's photograph and Ambertine's letter.

"By the tree outside your window," Grandpa mumbled, looking a little dazed. Then, slowly, he took the envelope from my hand. "What is this?" He frowned, opening it.

Grandpa glanced at the letter, eyes skitter-scatter. When he focused on the photograph, it was like he had the wind knocked out of him. "Joline," he whispered.

Grandpa put a hand against the door frame to steady himself, then, slowly, went inside.

When I followed, I found Grandpa in the sitting room, in the rocker by the fireplace. He was holding the picture like it was a robin's egg.

I sat down across from him, on the sofa.

"Where'd you get this?" All the snap had left his voice.

"Cousin Ambertine."

"Ambertine?" He squinted.

"She was here. The day of Aunt Tilley's funeral, after everybody left. When you took Cousin Richard to the depot."

"Ambertine, you say?" Grandpa looked addled. "Jake and Mamie's daughter?"

"Yes, Grandpa, and . . . what Ambertine told me and what Aunt Tilley told me about my ma and pa—things don't match up."

"This here letter from Ambertine?"

I nodded.

He looked at the letter, as if beholding a whirlwind, then handed it back to me. "What it say?"

Whenever Grandpa had me read him something from the newspaper, or Aunt Tilley a passage of Scripture, or Lawyer Sanders a document, I figured Grandpa wanted to see if I was a strong or weak reader, that he liked the way Aunt Tilley put drama in a verse, and that all lawyers read important papers aloud before people signed them.

Now that I thought about it, other than a hymnal at church, the only book I'd ever seen Grandpa handle was a ledger in which he did sums and such. I hardly ever saw him in the library. The few times I did, he looked lost in a forest.

"Dear Delana . . ." My voice trembled as I began reading Ambertine's letter. "Your mama had this picture taken years ago when she was up in Wheeling . . ." I paused now and then to read Grandpa's face.

He nodded when I read about Bethany and Miriam Rice and the freedom festivities.

After I read, "Up in Wheeling, that's where Joline met Jordan," Grandpa winced. And his eyes were glistening when I finished the part about my mother aiming to marry my father and have a vivid life.

"Ambertine said I should decide what I want, then signed off with 'Watching Over You.'"

"Watching over you?" Grandpa was riled up again.

"Before my mother died, she wrote Ambertine . . . asking her to watch over me. Ambertine gave me that note."

Now that envelope was in my outstretched hand. Quickly, I pulled it back.

"From Joline?" Grandpa was squinting again.

"Yessir."

"Let me see that."

I hesitated. He still had her picture. What if he never gave it back—kept her note, too?

But the anger was gone from his eyes.

I handed over the note. "It says, 'Keep watch over my baby girl.'"

He ran a finger over the purple maypops up top.

"Grandpa, Ambertine said my folks had a powerful love. Him for her. Her for him. And that my pa didn't truly run off, but faced a hard choice." By now, my eyes were on the carpet. "All I want is the truth, Grandpa."

"The truth?" His voice was low. "People like to talk about how truth set you free. Truth can come with burdens."

"But, Grandpa, is a burden worse than mystery?"

Our eyes locked. Soon, Grandpa's eyes were the ones on the carpet. A wave of weary washed over him. And he was traveling to the wayback of his mind.

"Delana, everything . . . this house, the shops, properties . . . all for family. My whole life's prayer was to do for mine what my ma and pa was denied."

Grandpa spoke of seeing his mama iron precious pinafores for the master's girls, while his sisters went about in rough and ratty tow-cloth shirts.

"Never forget my pa's hollow eyes when they brought him back hog-tied, bloody. He was to make it north, work at whatever he could, find a way to buy all our freedom."

I thought about Grandpa as a boy working hurry-scurry to buy his freedom.

"That was the second time my pa tried to escape. First time flogged. Second time hanged. All us colored on the plantation was made to watch. Then, my ma, sisters, brothers . . . we was all sold apart." He paused, then turned to me. "These some of my truths, Delana."

Grandpa went distant again.

"For family . . . all those years of stooping to conquer. . . . 'Yessir, Mr. Angus . . . Yessir, Mr. Smythe' . . . knowing it'd be a cold day in Hell before any of them put a 'Mister' before my name. . . . For family. I needed them white men to vouch for me when I wanted to open a shop, pick up a property. Needed the word to go out that Sam Hannibal was all right—for the rabble to know me and mine not to be harassed! For family. So my children could be strong masters of themselves. *Never* be scattered!"

Grandpa was awfully worked up. I feared for him. He'd never said a peep to me about slavery days and now things were just spilling out. What if it was more than he could bear?

I was relieved to see him looking close to peaceful as he drifted back to the days after the Civil War when he was seeking and searching for kinfolk—and sometimes finding family.

"Samuel Hannibal, formerly of Franklin County, Virginia, now in Charleston, West Virginia, looking for his sister Lavinia, who goes by Viney, once owned by Asa Meade.

"Samuel Hannibal, formerly of Franklin County, Virginia, now in Charleston, West Virginia, looking for his brother Jacob, also called Jake, once owned by Asa Meade."

Grandpa's voice grew stronger as he recited ads he had placed in newspapers, white and colored, forty years ago.

". . . looking for his sister Carrie, once owned by Asa Meade . . .

". . . looking for his sister Matilda, who goes by Tilley, once owned by Asa Meade . . .

". . . looking for his mother, Janie . . ."

Grandpa searched for second kin, too. "All I knew to do was cast a wide net."

Some kinfolk saw an ad with their own eyes, Grandpa said. Others heard one during times set aside by preachers and teachers for the reading of colored people's want ads.

Brothers, sisters, aunts, uncles, cousins—some sent Grandpa news of their whereabouts and plans to stay put. Others made their way to Charleston, but later fanned out. Only Uncle Jake and Aunt Tilley made Charleston home.

Grandpa said he never heard a word about what became of his mama. My heart scrunched up. And I thought about how many of Grandpa's truths were Aunt Tilley's truths, too.

"Meantime, Delia and I were making our own family." Grandpa's voice cracked. "Fever took the twins. Junior . . . too tight a taste for liquor, too much temper. Breathed his last on a filthy saloon floor . . ."

When Grandpa trailed off, he had a look on his face I'd never seen before.

A time or two right after Aunt Tilley died, I'd seen in Grandpa's eyes sadness, sorrow, but nothing like this, like he was trapped in a nightmare.

He was in pain.

I felt so sorry for Grandpa. Scared for him, too. Part of me wanted to tell him to stop.

"Junior not in the grave but a few months when I lost my Delia."

The way he said "my Delia" sounded like they, too, had a powerful love.

"Joline all I had left." Grandpa wiped his eyes as he went on to tell me how he gave my mother whatever she wanted. Pieces of jewelry. Bonnets. New bedroom suite—"Once a year even ordered her a whole crate of Chesapeake oysters.

"Was for her I added on that library." He had a slight smile. "Built the shelves where she wanted them, put up the wallpaper she picked out, let her purchase book after book, till all the shelves were filled like she wanted."

He looked at the photograph again.

"Never could say no to Joline. . . . Wish I had when she begged to go up to Wheeling."

His hands were trembling.

"When she come back, she couldn't stop talking about that fella. I tried to like him when he paid a visit, but couldn't see nothing in him but tumble-weed. Told Joline he'd never be able to offer her nothing but a hard life and a fish scale or two."

"Ambertine told me about my mother's fancy for three-cent silver," I broke in. "She gave me one." I lifted the hem of my skirt and took the tiny coin from its pocket.

Grandpa's eyes softened. I wondered if he was thinking of my mother and her three-cent silver every time he gave me silver dollars.

"Some of his letters carried one or two of them things." Grandpa scowled. "And her carrying on like he'd sent her a queen's diamond."

He couldn't even say my father's name. And the way he made it sound like my father wasn't worth spit—I didn't care if Grandpa took it as sass, I had to ask.

"Why were you so sure my father would never amount to—"

"He was working in a saloon—nothing to show for himself! A dreamer!"

"But that don't seem fair, Grandpa. Didn't you

once have nothing—and not even a claim on your own bones?"

Grandpa looked plumb perplexed.

"I'm just saying that . . . what Aunt Tilley told me about that man Hannibal Watson giving you a trade and freedom . . . is all that true?"

"All true, but—"

"And how you did things like sweep up saloons? . . . And later, after your freedom day, didn't you sleep in woods, in barns? But then got blessed to find a home where mercy abounded." I was crying again. "Where Grandma Delia lived—a house where mercy abounded! . . . Is that true?"

Grandpa nodded.

"Then why you couldn't let mercy abound in this house?"

"Your father wasn't nothing like me! I didn't steal Delia! I did things proper!"

Something shattered in the kitchen.

"No cause for alarm!" Miss Ida cried out. When she flustered into the sitting room, she begged pardon and explained why she'd come back.

"In all the commotion, I forgot to bring y'all a jar of my piccalilli to go with your supper. Then I saw a few dishes in the sink. Figured I'd wash them up right quick. Silly me let a teacup slip. But don't you worry, Mr. Hannibal, I shall replace it."

Grandpa held up his hand. "No need, Miss Nash," he sighed.

"So long as I'm here, be happy to get supper on the table."

Grandpa shook his head. "No need for all that. Just heat things up. We'll serve ourselves, take supper in the kitchen."

Grandpa rose from the rocker, handed me my mother's picture and her note, then left the room. His last angry words echoed in my head.

Your father wasn't nothing like me! I didn't steal Delia! I did things proper!

What did that mean? He made my father sound like some kind of fiend, a bandit. He stole my mother?

Why would he have to do that if they had a powerful love?

And your ma . . . she's got a power to her. That's what Adena had said. And Ambertine had talked about my mother's spirit—her fire. I couldn't see her letting anybody *steal* her.

None of this made sense. All sorts of things ran through my mind—like what Grandpa said happened to him when he didn't know where I was. *Quite a scare you give me. All sorts of things run through my mind.*

I saw the dazed look on Grandpa's face when I told him I'd left for Adena's by the tree outside my window. Then my mind traveled to that tree stump beneath my mother's bedroom window and how Ambertine said good-bye to my mother the night she lit out from Charleston.

From a tree like this one that used to be outside her window.

I hurried into the kitchen.

- - - - -

"She ran away?"

Grandpa was at the stove, putting a pork chop on a plate. Miss Ida was nowhere in sight, but a dish filled with piccalilli was in the middle of the kitchen table.

"Ran away with my father, didn't she?"

Grandpa put greens on the plate, then a piece of cornbread. He set the plate on the end of the table near where I stood.

The food was mud to me. I didn't sit at the table. I stood there. Waiting.

"She did," Grandpa finally said, swallowing hard. After another stretch of silence, he told me about the day Aunt Tilley came to The Traveler's Room all frantic and with a note my mother had left on her bed—"Papa, I love you, but I can't live without Jordan."

And about the telegram she sent a few days later—"Married. Will return if both can."

And about his fear—"No telling what hardships she might suffer, by the time she come to her senses."

And the telegram he sent back—"Come home. Both."

"They were up in Morgantown," Grandpa said. "I later learned that little hellion Ambertine was their witness. Didn't even know them two had kept in touch."

After my folks returned to Charleston, Grandpa gave my father a job, collecting rents and checking on shops.

"Was hoping some of my stability would rub off on him, but that fella stayed restless. Even when he knew your mama was expecting—he was still jawjacking about pulling up stakes soon as y'all strong enough to travel. Some foolishness about prospects in Alaska. I start to think he more than tumbleweed. He mad. Who with a baby on the way talk wild like that?"

"But, Grandpa, if he was going to take us both to Alaska, why did he leave before I was born?"

Grandpa hung his head. "He was here when you was born."

"But Aunt Tilley said— So was he here when my mother . . . ?"

"He the one seen her take her last breath."

"Did she live to, to hold me much?"

"Lived to hold you, lived to name you."

"Delana's not my true name?"

"It is. But nothing to do with Martin Delany. You half my Delia . . . half your father's mother. Ana."

Grandpa sat down at the kitchen table.

I sat down across from him, my mind a whirlwind.

"Joline wasn't in the ground a week when he start talking about moving on. With *you*. Wasn't going to let that happen! Couldn't lose you, too! Whatever it took—whatever I had to do."

I thought back to Grandpa as a boy sweeping saloons and doing whatever else he could to save up freedom money. And what he said to me every birthday.

Save your money, Delana. Don't spend it on trifles. Save for something dear.

I was horrified. "He sold me to you?"

Grandpa shook his head. "He bought you a future."

I was on my feet. "Bought me a future?" What in the world did that mean?

Grandpa wouldn't look at me. When he finally spoke, he still avoided my eyes. "Told him if he let you be mine, if he leave and never come back... when I go, everything—house, money in the bank, properties—all of it fall to you. He could go to Alaska—to Heaven, or Hell—knowing his daughter set for life."

Slowly, Grandpa rose, walked over to the kitchen window overlooking the back porch. "Had Lawyer Sanders draw up the papers. Had him put in, too, that if your father ever come within a mile, he'd make you a pauper. I wouldn't even leave you a fish scale."

The clock's ticktock was the only sound.

"Why you had to make it forever, Grandpa? Couldn't you give him a chance? Keep track of him—see if he turn stable? If he did, then . . . you could've given me back when you got tired of me."

Grandpa spun around, bewildered.

"Give you *back*? . . . *Tired of you*? Delana, you all that's left of my legacy."

I didn't know what it meant to be a legacy. All I knew was it had been a long time since Grandpa treated me like I was at all dear to him.

"Is my father still alive?" I didn't plead. I demanded.

"Don't know."

"Is that the truth, Grandpa?"

"God is my witness, Delana. I do not know if your father still walks the earth. "

"If he does and I find out where and go within a mile of him, will you cast me out?"

- - - - -

"Delana."

I had run out onto the back porch. I had been balled up in the porch swing for I don't know how long when Grandpa called me from the kitchen.

I wished it was colder. Cold enough to freeze to death.

The second time Grandpa called my name he was in the doorway looking bone-weary, his voice strangely soft.

"Something for you to see. Up in your room."

Eleven

The rug beneath where the attic ladder lets down was littered with splinters and bits of plaster. In my room, near the foot of my bed, was a dusty carpetbag.

"Most of her trinkets and keepsakes . . . in that there bag."

Grandpa was downstairs, likely in The Traveler's Room, before I even moved.

I wished I could roll back the days. Wished I had screamed when Ambertine took her hand from over my mouth. She would have skedaddled, never come near me again. Or when she gave me a choice—

If you fear me, I will leave. If not, hear me out,

Delana, and with the knowing part of your soul. . . .
Your choice.

Instead of "Stay," I should've said "Go!"

Then my life would've been like always. Me just standing by, waiting to be told what to do and with nothing to fear but closing my eyes when dragon-flies were near.

Decide what you want, Delana.

A vanity set—mirror, brush, comb. These were the first things I lifted from the dusty carpetbag, so much of me hoping that even without my own firsthand memories—even without knowing the sound of her voice or how sly or brightly she smiled—maybe I could get to know her, feel her . . . have some of my mother come to me by getting to know her things.

Next, a jewelry box. Every piece silver. Eardrops. Stickpins, one topped with a maypop.

There was also a neck chain and three pendants—a heart, a shell, a crescent moon.

From a black leather change purse, I counted out thirty-three three-cent silver.

There were letters, too. One bundle, tied with a bright green ribbon, was from Miss Bertha Mason in Chicago, Kansas City, St. Louis, Philadelphia,

New York, Boston, Morgantown, Gallipolis, New Orleans.

Another batch—blue ribbon this time—was from other people. Some names I recognized as family.

No letters from Jordan Burkett.

Had Grandpa known my father's letters by sight? Or maybe he had Aunt Tilley sort them out so he could burn them or tear them up in a thousand tiny pieces. Making my father disappear. Like he did on my mother's gravestone.

Joline *Burkett*—not Joline *Hannibal!*—that's what it should say. Just like, by rights, my name wasn't Delana *Hannibal*.

I was Delana *Burkett*.

Had Grandpa destroyed every trace of my father? I wondered as I skimmed through a packet of articles from the *Daily Gazette*, the *Christian Recorder*, and other newspapers. Some articles had people's names underlined. None my father's, so I didn't even read them.

Only one clipping got my full attention. It was from the *Wheeling Intelligencer*. September 23, 1891.

Your mama had this picture taken years ago when she was up in Wheeling . . .

Sure enough, this clipping was a memento from what my mother called her first "on my own."

FITTINGLY OBSERVED.

The Celebration of Emancipation
Day a Success.

B. K. BRUCE'S ELOQUENT SPEECH

Enthusiastically Received by a Fine
Audience, and he Talks Sound Sense—
The Parade Attractive and Imposing,
and the Town Generally in Holiday
Garb.

The day was "bright and warm," said the newspaper, and "by 10 o'clock the streets were thronged with colored and white."

The parade—it went on and on. Mayor, chief marshals, police, a hook and ladder truck, a wagon of little girls representing the states of the union, a brass band, even twelve horsemen, along with streams of hacks and buggies all decked out.

I conjured up my mother among all these proud paraders. I saw her in a glorious pearly white dress and a glamorous hat—with lace and purple maypops. She was smiling, laughing, cheering, with her friends Bethany and Miriam, all three waving hankies or flags.

Maybe when her buggy passed the saloon, my father was standing outside. She caught his eye and he threw off his apron and joined the parade.

Reading on, and hoping to see mention of my mother's name, of my father's, I imagined my mother and her friends hurrying—running—to the fairgrounds, and my father following fast behind them, then getting as near to her as he could during the oration of the Honorable Blanche K. Bruce.

I knew him. After Hiram Revels, Blanche K. Bruce was the next of the race to be a United States senator. Aunt Tilley had a special affection for Mr. Bruce. Like her and Grandpa, he had come through slavery in Virginia.

Mr. Bruce was in a print above the fireplace in the parlor.

"Heroes of the Colored Race."

In the center, most prominent, was Mr. Bruce, Frederick Douglass, and Hiram Revels.

During our visits to kinfolk, when Aunt Tilley and I reached the fireplace, she didn't only greet

HEROES OF THE COLORED RACE.

family on the mantel. She looked up and spoke to the Heroes of the Colored Race.

"Good day, Mr. Bruce, Mr. Douglass, Mr. Revels," she'd say, then salute other men in the print. "Father Abraham . . . General Grant . . . Mr. Brown."

"Heroes of the Colored Race" probably hung in the very same spot when my mother was a girl. Seeing Mr. Bruce in the flesh must have been such a special treat for her.

I imagined her getting all choked up when he spoke about the pride and purpose of Emancipation Day, saying how it should be as dear to us as the Fourth of July. "Kindred anniversaries," he called them. "The one marks the birth of a nation and the other of a race."

Right there, *I* got all choked up. But it wasn't over memories of yearly celebrations in school and church of the twenty-second of September 1862, when Abraham Lincoln announced he'd soon set people in slavery free. Nor was I remembering festivities in honor of the first of January 1863, when Lincoln sent out to all creation the Emancipation Proclamation. What had me about to cry had nothing to do with Father Abraham at all. But with Grandpa.

How he savored that rabbit stew we had every first of August. His freedom day.

No kin with him to celebrate back then.

I thought about Grandpa again when I read what Mr. Bruce said to the crowd about the need for colored to work hard and have property.

Grandpa had done just that, coming up from slavery. After seeing his pa killed, with his ma lost to him forever, then the family he made in freedom ... I thought about all his truths, all he had been through. I saw that pain on his face.

And now Aunt Tilley was gone, too.

I was the closest kin left to him.

Your grandpa done sounded the alarm, got folks searching for you! That's what Miss Lottie had said.

If he didn't care about me, Grandpa would've been in the sitting room playing checkers with himself. But when Miss Lottie brought me home, he had his traveling clothes on. He must've been about to go search for me himself.

And the way Jude hollered out when he saw me—
She found, Mr. Hannibal. She found.

Sounded like Jude and the whole wide world knew I was dear to Grandpa.

Couldn't lose you, too!

I wiped tears from my eyes.

Grandpa came to mind some more when I read Mr. Bruce's remarks on the import of saving money—and how he chided an old colored man who shucked that off.

"Great heavens," said Mr. Bruce to the man, "if you are too old to save for your own benefit, think of posterity!"

I wondered if posterity was the same as legacy.

For family.

I remembered Grandpa's slight smile when he talked about adding the library for my mother's sake. More likely than not, the whole house was for family's sake. That must've been why he was content with The Traveler's Room. Grandpa was the kind of man Mr. Bruce would've been proud to know. I couldn't help but smile.

But then, my heart sank as I read Mr. Bruce's stern words to young women about picking a husband.

```
Tell the young man he must be
industrious, be sober, strive for
knowledge, if he would wed you. Do
not marry a dude.
```

A dude? Sounded like the kind of man Grandpa said my father was.

Tumbleweed.

I didn't want to read anymore. So I set the article aside.

The next thing I took from the carpetbag was a book, done up with a red ribbon even though it wasn't falling apart.

"Sketches of Southern Life," I read when I opened the book.

By Frances E. Watkins Harper.

A page on, in plain hand, was written:

For My Beloved Joline,

You are my poem.

Everlasting Love,
Jordan

Tears rolled down my cheek. For her. For him. Tears for me.

At last, I had something of my father.

My hands were shaking as I leafed through this book of what seemed to be all poems. I soon saw why *Sketches of Southern Life* had been ribboned up.

In between two pages was a tintype of a man.

I didn't need to study it. Didn't need to wonder.

The tears were hot and fast.

This had to be my father.

Twelve

I wanted to be in a never-ending dream.

I wanted to be in my room on a golden day, reading a book or writing a poem when Miss Ida would rap on my door.

"Delana, my dear, you have a visitor!" Then she'd hurry me down to the parlor, where she had everything laid out for tea. And there, sitting on the red velvet settee with Grandpa—my father.

"I've been on an adventure!" he'd say.

"All's forgiven," Grandpa would chime in. "All's right with the world."

But nothing was right in my world.

I was sitting up in my bed, still in yesterday's clothes, hugging myself under my quilt.

I tiptoed over to my window.

It was barely first light. Some of the moon was still showing through. Far off a cock crowed. Closer, a dog let out a wounded howl.

I picked up my father's picture from my bureau.

Why did he choose scenery with a tree? Was this photograph taken before they met? If after, was he looking off to the side like that because he was looking at my mother?

But wouldn't my folks have had a picture taken together after they married up in Morgantown?

Grandpa. There had to have been other pictures. Grandpa had destroyed them. All my forgiveness feelings were fading.

Grandpa was *wrong* about my father, *wrong* about him being tumbleweed. All these years Jordan Burkett had been working hard—as hard as he could. He had struck gold in Alaska or become prosperous somehow else in a faraway land. Right now he was on his way to West Virginia, to Charleston, right up to the front door of this house! Coming to get me and to tell Grandpa to give his legacy to somebody else!

I looked at my father's picture again. Had

Grandpa been right? Would I have had an awfully wretched life? Ended up a ragamuffin?

He bought you a future.

Maybe my father knew I couldn't bear up under a tumbleweed life.

But what would happen to me after Grandpa died? What would I do with the legacy? Me run barbershops? How would I know how much rent to make people pay?

Maybe I'd ask Lawyer Sanders to handle things, if he wasn't dead, too, then I'd travel around, visiting kinfolk for real. Bring Adena with me. She wouldn't have to do chores and errands anymore. I'd pay Miss Ida and Jude to help Miss Lottie.

Better yet, I'd tell Adena her family could move in here with me. Also Miss Ida. Save her a lot of back and forth. Jude, too. I once heard Miss Ida say Jude don't half live no place but among hoot owls and ramps. Jude could have The Traveler's Room.

If I couldn't fill up the house ... I couldn't imagine nothing for myself but getting old and crazy. Spending my days in the sitting room making doilies and in the parlor conjuring up stories about photographs. And I didn't even have a wishing-place, a place to say my dreams.

I closed my eyes. I imagined myself walking down to the Kanawha River, knowing in my soul which was the welcoming tree.

Father God, I prayed, *please don't let me be miserable all my life. Let the sorrow lift.*

I wished I was back in the Bible days, when prayers moved God to do miracle things. Seas parted. Walls came tumbling down. Dry bones lived.

Nothing like that happened for me.

When I opened my eyes, I was beholding the same sad sky. And that elm outside my window no longer looked like a sturdy black hand, a rescue. It was just a tree.

- - - - -

My days were like snails in the darkness. Parts of my heart . . . nibbled away. During recess and after school, I didn't even have much to say to Adena.

Only one bright spot—Viola Kimbrough had stopped nettling me. The teasing of Adena had also eased.

The turnaround came the day I had to recite. I rose slowly, prepared my mind. From across the aisle came the ghosty voice, "Dumb . . . Delana."

I turned to Viola. "Why don't you just hush up!"

The class roared.

Viola cut her eyes at me.

"And keep your nasty eyes to yourself while you're at it!"

Again, the class broke out in laughter. Viola slunk down in her seat.

When I faced front, I figured I'd find a furious Miss Tolliver, but she looked like she was doing her utmost not to laugh, too.

"Class, settle down now," she finally said, then, "proceed, Delana, proceed."

I did. Only it wasn't the poem Miss Tolliver had assigned. I didn't understand this new poem any more than the other one, but this poem was dear to me. It was the one my father's picture faced.

I cleared my throat. "'I Thirst' by Frances E. Watkins Harper."

Miss Tolliver seemed surprised but not riled. "Yes, Delana, go on."

I thirst, but earth cannot allay
    The fever coursing through my veins;
The healing stream is far away—
    It flows through Salem's lovely plains.

The murmurs of its crystal flow
    Break ever o'er this world of strife;
My heart is weary, let me go,
    To bathe it in the steam of life;

For many worn and weary hearts
    Have bathed in this pure healing stream,
And felt their griefs and cares depart,
    E'en like some sad forgotten dream.

- - - - -

"Good morning."

"Good night."

Some days those were the only words that passed between Grandpa and me. Suppertimes were horrible. Him at the head of the dining room table. Me at the side. Us eating to the whip of the wind or the clock's ticktock until one of us said, "Pass the cornbread, please."

I'd gotten used to being alone upstairs. Had come to the conclusion I'd just have to mother myself.

Sleeping in my mother's room helped some. Often, before I went to sleep, I looked at the pictures of my folks, searching their faces for clues to me.

Sometimes I fiddled with my mother's things from that carpetbag. Put on a neck chain. Hold her eardrops up to my face.

Reading my mother's letters from friends and family, I was starting to piece together more of her personality. She liked to bake pies, to dance, and to talk about the books she read. And she was fond of saying *Pshaw!*

My next comfort was being in her library. I did my needlework there—and no more primroses for me! I was stitching stars. Sometimes moons, with plans to tackle purple maypops soon.

I'd also decided to do a whole lot of reading in the library, starting with *Jane Eyre*, a little bit every day.

Didn't know which book I'd pick up next.

Emma?

The Wide, Wide World?

Or maybe *The Way We Live Now* or *Uncle Tom's Cabin* or *The Count of Monte Cristo* or *Bleak House* or *Life and Public Services of Martin R. Delany*.

All I knew was a burning desire to read every book my mother put on those shelves.

It was also in the library that I began bringing some order to the kinfolk. Matching up husbands and wives, sisters and brothers, noting what I knew and what I wondered.

Like the man Aunt Tilley had just called "Top-hat." Uncle Dub's brother, if I remembered correctly.

And there were the Dowds. Three sisters and a brother. All four took their picture against the same scene. The ghosty house in the distance never made sense. It looked a little like Adena's house, but the Dowds looked prosperous. Maybe they posed with that house as a show of modesty.

What else were they trying to say about themselves by what they picked to pose with? I most liked the brother's fetching kerchief placed over the tree stump. Maybe he was a magician.

A frightful feeling came over me. Was this how it started with Aunt Tilley? When she couldn't remember or didn't know or didn't like a truth, she just made things up?

I was going to start from scratch.

- - - - -

"Grandpa?"

I had the Dowds with me when I went into the sitting room. Grandpa was playing checkers with himself.

"Who are these people?" I asked.

The Dowds, he said, were some of Grandma Delia's people.

"Where do they live?"

"Toledo."

"Is he a magician?"

"Magician? No, preacher. Big church."

I ran back to the library for Aunt Tilley's husband, Uncle Dub, and Tophat. Maybe they weren't brothers. They didn't much favor.

Grandpa said Tophat *was* Uncle Dub's brother, Thomas. "Butler for a judge in Richmond."

"Uncle Dub? Was that his real name?"

"No. Double. Something to do with his time of birth."

I was headed back to the library for another picture when Grandpa asked, "What is it that you're up to, Delana?"

I feared a scolding, but then saw Grandpa didn't look cross.

"Unscrambling family. Just want to know who is who."

"You'll wear yourself out you keep running back and forth like that. Could just bring the whole lot in here."

Grandpa and I began spending evenings together in the sitting room visiting kinfolk.

I learned that Grandma's sister, Aunt Rachel, wasn't a floozy, but a poet, making me like the way she decorated herself even more.

As for Cousin Eula, she really was Emma!

"Remember Clare who came to the funeral?"

How could I forget Ole Weepy?

"Emma her baby sister. They Ambertine's cousins, on her mama's side."

I was also glad to hear that Emma wasn't dead. And not passing for white. Grandpa said it was another sister, Lena, who did that.

I turned Emma's photograph over. "And this Pearlie Bruce who Emma gave her picture to?"

"Used to board with Jake and Mamie."

"Was Pearlie Bruce kin to Blanche K. Bruce?"

"Not to my knowledge."

But Grandpa did know for sure that we were no kin to Martin Delany.

"That was Tilley being fanciful." Grandpa sighed. "Strange as she got, would rather have her with us still than not."

- - - - -

That's just what I was thinking on Christmas Day—Aunt Tilley.

Grandpa and I were in the parlor ready to exchange gifts.

Miss Ida was in the kitchen. For Christmas dinner, on top of the roast turkey and ham and yams and rice and cowpeas and greens, we were having roast duck, and rabbit, a goose, mashed potatoes, stuffing, and oyster soup. Enough for five families! Lawyer Sanders would go home with enough food to last him *days*. Ever since his wife died, he took holiday meals with us.

Back when Grandpa asked Miss Ida how much money she needed for Christmas dinner, she said, "Not a cent, Mr. Hannibal. All this year's Christmas doings is my gift to you and Delana."

Miss Ida had always given us decorations for the tree. This year she had gone above and beyond on that count. Along with the popcorn string, paper angels, and fringed foil for the tree, we had store-bought baubles and stars for the first time. There was also holly and wreaths all over the house—and a big bowl of candy on the parlor's lion's paw table. All this on top of so much food.

I wondered what had come over Miss Ida to

make her so generous. Was she trying to make up for letting that teacup slip?

Later I'd give Miss Ida hankies with moons and stars. And when Grandpa and I made the rounds, I'd be giving Adena some hankies, too. But right now it was gift-giving time for me and Grandpa.

"Me first," I said.

In Christmases past, Aunt Tilley wrapped up some socks for me to give Grandpa. This year when I handed him a little package, the gift really was from me.

He looked puzzled but pleased when he lifted the fifty-cent piece from the red velvet pouch.

"Cousin Richard gave it to me. Prettiest one I've ever seen. So I want you to have it."

"This will be a most prized possession." Grandpa looked so happy. "Thank you, Delana."

Then he handed me a package. "From Tilley. Put it by for you months ago."

It was a beautiful white blouse with a touch of lace, not like for a child but for a girl growing up.

Your day will come. That's what Aunt Tilley had said.

Even with all her fancifuls . . . all her bewares, I was wishing she was with us still. Things would be different now. I had some truths.

Then I remembered something Ambertine had said.

When I got word she was gone, I decided it was time for you to know some things, get some freedom wings.

If Aunt Tilley hadn't died, who knows when Ambertine would've come into my life.

When I looked at Grandpa, there was so much tenderness in his eyes. Then he held me in his arms. "Go ahead," he said, "let it out. Let it all out."

It was a bigger cry than the night Aunt Tilley died, a deeper cry than when I first laid eyes on my mother's likeness. My tears were hotter than when I found my father's picture in that book.

There was still so much I didn't understand, so much more I wanted to know, but mostly I was feeling so sorry for hating Aunt Tilley. And Grandpa.

How many more years would I have him? That brought on a new wave of tears. If talk about my father caused Grandpa harm, I'd bide my time. I never again wanted to see that pain in his eyes.

Your day will come.

I wasn't hearing Aunt Tilley this time. I was spirit-speaking to myself.

"Delana," Grandpa said softly. "Been a rough

patch for you, I know. And, no doubt, you been wrestling with some hard-hearted feelings about Tilley. About me, too. . . . Things Tilley told you . . . was from fear. Fear there'd come a day you'd want to know about your father, try to find him. Leave us."

My tears had eased up, but Grandpa was still holding me. "I let Tilley tell you what she wished because I was afraid, too. And I'm sorry, Delana." Grandpa swallowed. "Sorry, too, for not letting you know how dear you are to me. So busy protecting you, so afraid of losing you . . . I made you too dear."

I looked up, confused.

"What I mean is, I wanted you walled off from anything I thought might bring you harm or hurt. Only way I could do that was to stand guard outside the wall myself. . . . Older you got the higher the wall I thought was needed." Grandpa wiped his eyes. "Ain't a right way to live. Not for you. Not for me."

I felt tears on the rise again.

I also felt the sorrow lift.

The scent of cinnamon filled the room. We were also having peach cobbler. And sweet potato pie. Red velvet cake, too. I hoped all that cooking didn't send Miss Ida into a faint. She'd been working on Christmas dinner for a week.

And Grandpa was now handing me my Christmas gift from him.

It was a big beautiful photograph album! On the shiny cream cover was a dance of yellow-faced pansies.

"Oh, thank you, Grandpa! Thank you so much!"

"Family been in that basket long enough, don't you think?"

We both started laughing. Nothing was truly funny, but it felt good. So we laughed some more.

I stopped when Grandpa brought out a photograph from his jacket pocket.

A photograph of him!

"Was going through some old papers when I come across this," he said, handing it to me.

The photograph was taken, I saw, where Aunt Tilley once sat in a chair that brought to mind a throne. Where she was wearing her white festivity hat. Shadle & Busser. In York, Pennsylvania.

"You think it's too chewed up to rate a place in that new album of your'n?" Grandpa asked with a slight smile. "Maybe I can have it fixed up."

"No need, Grandpa. No need. It's perfect."

- - - - -

Soon, Grandpa was saying "No" a lot less.

When I asked Miss Ida if I could help her cook and she said, "You need to ask your grandpa," he gave his consent—and with a big sunshine smile, too!

They were both amazed at how well I knew my way around the kitchen—stirring pots, frying eggs and bacon, peeling potatoes, grinding coffee, baking pies. A lot had stuck from all those years of watching.

Then came the Friday in February when Grandpa mentioned, over supper, that he was going down to Malden to see about a property in the morning.

"Can I come?"

I not only got to see Malden. A few weeks later, Grandpa let me go with him to check on a shop in Boone County. And there, Grandpa had all the barbers come out to the buggy, then introduced me like I was mighty dear to him.

One of the barbers, Mr. Adams, looked a little like Adena's father. During the ride home, I asked Grandpa if Mr. Adams was Melungin and if they were people to beware.

Grandpa said Mr. Adams was a fine barber and an honest man. "Wouldn't care if his people from the moon."

As the buggy rolled by a stand of sugar maples, with some old men tapping for sap, I asked Grandpa something else to do with my friend. "Can Adena come to the house sometimes, spend time with me?"

Grandpa said "Yes" to that, too.

- - - - -

"I know, Grandpa. Save my money. Don't spend it on trifles. Save for something dear."

That was on another Friday, the second of March. My thirteenth birthday.

We were in the sitting room and Grandpa had just counted out thirteen silver dollars into my hands.

"Thank you," I said, giving him a peck on the cheek.

"There's something else," he said, patting the spot next to him.

As I sat down, Grandpa rubbed his chin, drummed his fingers on his knee.

"You all right, Grandpa?"

"I'm fine," he said, but he still didn't look it. "Want to speak on a question you asked me a while back. Right then and there I answered my heart but . . . never did answer you."

Grandpa lifted my chin so we were eye to eye. "Delana, there's nothing in the world you could ever do to make me cast you out. And I include in that . . . you going within a mile of your father . . . or him coming within a foot of you."

I froze.

"When I said I didn't know if he was still alive, that was the honest truth, but that didn't mean I couldn't try and find out." After a pause, he added, "I did like I did after the war . . . when I was trying to find family."

Did I hear right? Was Grandpa saying he had placed want ads for my father?

Yes, he had.

". . . looking for Jordan Burkett, for a time of Wheeling, West Virginia. Mother named Ana."

A tear rolled down my cheek.

Grandpa had Lawyer Sanders place the ads, pretending they were from somebody who thought my father might be kin. For the reply address, he used a friend's in Roanoke. Grandpa said he preferred my father not know just yet that he was the one looking for him.

"A reply come the other week."

I could hardly speak. "My father's alive?"

"Seemed so." Grandpa hugged me to him. "But I wanted to know so. Had Lawyer Sanders go see, check around. When need be he can walk through snow leaving nary a track."

"Where'd you send Lawyer Sanders?"

"Baltimore."

Alaska, that's what I expected to hear. If not Alaska, then some other faraway place, with oceans and mountains, maybe even deserts, between here and there.

But Baltimore was near.

"Is he still . . . tumbleweed?"

"No, Delana. Seems he made out good. Tailor. Have his own little shop."

"Does he have any . . . other . . . children?"

Grandpa shook his head.

"Wife?"

"Don't seem he ever married again."

From his vest pocket, Grandpa pulled out a piece of paper, pressed it in my hand. "What more you want to know, you can ask him yourself."

I unfolded the paper, stared at the address. "I can write him?"

"Yes, Delana, if you want to. Your choice."

"Thank you, Jesus!"

We turned to see Miss Ida standing in the archway.

"Bless your heart, Mr. Hannibal," she continued, fighting back tears. "It's been such a joy to see you stop making Delana live such a locked-up life. And now this. Finding her father."

Something in my spirit flipped. That phrase "locked-up life"—I'd heard it before.

This locked-up life ain't what your mama would want for you.

That was something Ambertine had said.

Queer things suddenly made sense, like pieces of a jigsaw puzzle coming to fit. Starting with how fidgety Miss Ida looked when she told me to hurry to my room after Aunt Tilley's funeral.

Best go upstairs and rest yourself awhile. . . . Hurry now, hurry.

And when I got to my room—

I sprang to my feet, arms akimbo. "Miss Ida— you been Ambertine's spy?"

Miss Ida lowered her eyes and fiddled with her hands.

Grandpa's mouth fell open.

That's how Ambertine knew Aunt Tilley called her "Trash and trouble."

Miss Ida!

How Ambertine knew I liked geography and knew other things about me.

Miss Ida!

When I got word she was gone, I decided it was time for you to know some things, get some freedom wings.

Miss Ida!

Grandpa looked from Miss Ida to me, from me to Miss Ida, who finally fessed up.

To sending Ambertine reports on me like she'd asked her to do years ago.

To sending Ambertine word that Aunt Tilley had died.

To sneaking Ambertine into the house the night of the funeral.

To putting Ambertine's letter on my bed.

To eavesdropping the evening Grandpa told me all those truths.

"True," Miss Ida added, her eyes still on her hands, "I saw Ambertine as a strange one, but I never felt her evil. When she said Delana's father didn't merit everlasting banishment and damnation, seemed to me there was something to it. With all due respect, Mr. Hannibal, you was a stubborn man and hard-hearted for too long."

Now it was Grandpa who lowered his eyes.

"And for the record," Miss Ida continued, "I never asked Ambertine for a dime, but over the years, I did accept her freewill offerings. But I swear, Mr. Hannibal, every cent I spent on y'all's Christmases."

That explained why Miss Ida had lavished so much on us this Christmas.

"And I'll spare you the trouble of telling me my services are no longer needed. I'll get supper on the table, clean up, then never darken your door again."

Grandpa looked as he did when working in his ledger book, like he was adding and subtracting in his head.

I looked at my father's address again, then at Miss Ida. "Ambertine knew all along where my father was, didn't she?"

Miss Ida nodded. "She said all she could do was plant a seed and see what grows." Then Miss Ida turned to Grandpa. "Had she come to you, Mr. Hannibal, she figured you wouldn't give her a hearing, what with her being a family outcast."

Grandpa rubbed his chin. "She figured right." Then he brightened. "But this is a new day. Where's Ambertine now?"

"I don't rightly know," Miss Ida replied. "Only know how to get a message to her."

"And you'll be giving her a new report, I suspect."

Miss Ida's reply was a quick nod and a nervous smile.

"When you do, I want you to give her a message from me. We can talk about it later."

Miss Ida turned to leave the room.

"And one more thing, Miss Nash."

She stopped.

"I want to thank you for your service. All of it. And you were right. About a lot of things." Grandpa got fidgety, drumming his fingers on his knee. "It would please me greatly if when you set the table, you set a place for yourself, have supper with me and Delana."

Miss Ida was beaming. She bounced from the room.

Grandpa had a nice smile on his face. I couldn't help but ask, "You getting sweet on Miss Ida?"

"You think I should be?"

I nodded. "And Grandpa . . . ?"

"Yes, Delana?"

"Your message to Ambertine . . . you'll tell her she's welcome here?"

"You think that's what I should do?"

"Yes!"

"Me too. I want mercy to abound in this house." Grandpa gave himself a good stretch. "First thing tomorrow, going to see Lawyer Sanders. Have him draw up some new papers."

Grandpa looked down at the paper in my hand. "And what are you going to do?"

Thirteen

As I lay in bed that night, in my head I started writing letter after letter to Mr. Jordan Burkett in Baltimore, Maryland.

Dear Father,
  I trust this letter finds you well. I am doing fine....

Dear Father,
  I still live in the house on Shrewsbury Street....

Dear Father,
  Your head must be spinning like a top....

Dear Father God, I prayed, *show me what to write. Show me how not to worry.*

I worried that my father might not write back. Or that if he did, he'd say he didn't want to see me.

And what if he and Grandpa never made peace?

Suddenly, Uncle Matthias's picture postcard was in my head. But this time, I didn't get all panicky when I put myself in the railroad scene.

I felt like that train would take the curve just fine. When it reached the other side of the mountain, I still didn't know what I'd see, but I didn't fear an abyss.

Next, I saw myself in Cousin Clare's postcard, on Market Street. I was looking in all the shop windows, and I saw a lot of things I liked. And that's when it hit me.

While I was wrestling with what to write my father, there was something else I needed to do.

I made up my mind to do it the next day.

- - - - -

"Miss Ida?" I called out on my way down the front stairs. I knew Grandpa wasn't home. After breakfast, he had gone to see Lawyer Sanders.

"In here," Miss Ida replied from the parlor. She and Jude were moving furniture to the walls. Next, he'd be carrying the rugs out back for beating.

Jude looked at me once. Then again.

"My, my," said Miss Ida.

I had on one of my church skirts, best bonnet, and, most dear to me, Aunt Tilley's Christmas blouse.

"Miss Ida, I am going out."

"Where to?"

"Not far."

"Does your grandpa know?"

"No. That's why I'm telling you, Miss Ida. So nobody sounds the alarm."

With that, I left home with a pocketful of silver dollars.

My first on my own.

I wasn't going as far as my mother had gone, but it was a start.

- - - - -

Capitol Street was beehive busy. People going in and out of shops, some fast, some slow. Others crowded around carts piled high with fruits and vegetables and around a peddler covered in kazoos.

Up ahead a ways, a dog yapped. Closer, a baby squalled—and only a couple of colored on the street.

I'd never been all alone around so many white folks.

Thump-thump.

But as none looked like they would do me harm, I calmed down, strolled on. And it was easy to mosey.

So much to see.

The few times Aunt Tilley took me shopping with her, she never let me linger at a store window like McCrory's, chock-full of shining china, glittering glassware, crystal birds, tin toy soldiers, and other playthings, including a golden teddy bear.

Farther along, I came to Friedman's. There, a girl not much older than me was neatening up a mannequin in a peach satin gown. When I looked at my reflection, I was bothered by my bonnet. I wanted to see myself in a different kind of hat, something akin to the one my mother had on in that photograph.

The girl in the window smiled.

I went inside to find that of all the hats in Friedman's, only one came close.

"For you?" the saleslady asked.

"Yes'm."

"Maybe a little too old?" She peered at me over her glasses.

"No disrespect, ma'am, but I . . . I like it."

When I left Friedman's, I only lingered at a few more shop windows—Stromboni's ice cream parlor, Sterret's grocery, Bogg's pharmacy.

I walked fast by the saloon and didn't slow down until I reached Gates Art Gallery.

A whole lot of hubbub inside. People oohing and aahing and hmmming over oil paintings up on a long stretch of wall and in bold, gold frames. Some of every kind of scene. A castle with turrets piercing clouds . . . sheep in a peaceful valley . . . people enjoying a picnic in a park. The woman standing closest to that picnic painting had a measuring tape in her hand.

Up on the other side of the room, I saw a man and a little boy coming down the stairs. At the counter, a skinny sour-faced clerk talked sharp and fast to the man. I couldn't make out everything, but I did hear the clerk say, "Four dollars for the first. One dollar for each copy." And then, "Darkroom's a little backed up. Your order will be ready on Monday afternoon." The clerk told the man he had to leave a two-dollar deposit.

I never knew there was so much business to do around getting your picture taken.

Just then, a man in a gray smock came down the stairs. When he reached the desk behind the counter, he tended to some paperwork. He looked up when someone called out, "Mr. Gates!"

It was the woman before the picnic in the park painting. And now I knew the man in the gray smock was Mr. Gates.

"Will you do me a kindness," the woman asked him. "Hold this painting for me? I'll come for it next Friday."

"Will do, Mrs. Moore."

"Next!" the clerk called out.

When I turned, Sourface was looking at me, and I saw the spirit of Viola Kimbrough in him.

Thump-thump.

I tried to smile as I moved to the counter. "I came to get my picture taken."

"What time is your appointment?"

Lawdamercy! I paused, lowered my eyes. "I don't have an appointment, sir."

Sourface flipped through a book. "Wednesday afternoon . . . at four."

So much for my first on my own, I thought. "Yessir. Thank you."

"Name?"

"Delana"

"Spell that."

I did.

"Surname?"

I hesitated, but not for long. "Hannibal. Delana Hannibal."

Now Mr. Gates looked at me. "You kin to Sam Hannibal?"

No spirit of Viola Kimbrough in him!

"Yessir. He's my grandfather."

"When's my next appointment?" Mr. Gates asked the clerk.

Sourface looked at the book, then at his pocket watch. "About another forty minutes," he replied.

"Then I can take the young miss," said Mr. Gates.

- - - - -

Gates's upper room was a wonderland. Sunshine flooded in from a skylight. In one corner was a table and chair set up like two were having tea.

Nearby was an armchair, side table, bear rug—a little sitting room.

With a fireplace, too. A shelf up above was

a clutter of candlesticks, hurricane lamps, urns, vases, big and little baskets, shields, Ali Baba hats, and a parade of knickknacks.

The camera faced the fireplace. It was fixed on a cart with wheels and draped with a cloth. Made me think of the story about the Trojan horse. A Trojan horse with a little cape.

"What kind of scene do you fancy, young miss?" Mr. Gates asked. He pointed to the back of the room, where I saw huge paintings, from one of woodlands to one of a sea with sailboats in the distance.

"No scene, sir."

"Props?" Now he pointed to the big baskets in front of the scenes, baskets overflowing with books and scrolls, feathers and fans, hats, spears, parasols, umbrellas.

I shook my head. "No props. Just me."

"Then just you it'll be," he said with a smile.

Mr. Gates pulled over a dark screen, had me stand before it, then faced the camera at me.

Such a big eye.

I stood as straight as I could.

"Not yet. You can relax."

He ducked under the cloth, fiddled with the

camera. When his head popped back out—"Look straight at the camera. And now's the time to stay still. Don't blink, don't move."

So I stood there before the big eye. I stood there eyes wide open, not breathing deep, hoping I didn't look severe or sassy.

When you turn thirteen, Delana, you'll be getting your picture taken at Gates . . . when you turn thirteen.

Aunt Tilley had been right. And as I thought back, it dawned on me that she never said *she* would be taking me to Gates. Only that I'd be here.

How did she know?

Could it be that despite all her twitchy and strange ways, in the knowing part of her soul Aunt Tilley saw a change was coming for me? After all, she put by a grown-up blouse for me months ago. Maybe there was a part of her not bedeviled by fears and bewares that wanted me to get some freedom wings. Was that Aunt Tilley's last wish?

The camera's flash had me blinking fast.

"Done!" Mr. Gates beamed.

On my way downstairs, I counted in my head. *Grandpa . . . Miss Ida . . . Adena . . . Ambertine . . .*

"Six copies," I said to the clerk, then asked, "They'll be ready Monday afternoon?"

To my surprise, Sourface smiled. When I brought out two silver dollars, he waved his hand. "No need for a deposit. You can just pay when you pick up."

- - - - -

On the way back down Capitol Street, something caught my eye in a tiny bookshop I hadn't noticed before.

"How much is the globe?" I asked the little old man inside.

"Which? Terrestrial or celestial?"

I bit my lip. "Beg pardon?"

The man pointed to the globe in the window, one like we had in school. "Terrestrial. It maps the earth," he said. "Four dollars." Then he pointed to a shelf behind the counter, and to a smaller globe I hadn't noticed. It was deep-sea blue with bright white stars and strange creatures in gold. "Celestial. Maps the heavens. Five dollars."

"I'll take the celestial," I said.

While the man wrapped up my globe, I looked around at all the books on shelves that lined the room. I wondered if this bookshop was here when my mother was alive.

Then I noticed a rack of picture postcards. Most were scenes from Charleston.

Capitol Street. Kanawha Street. The depot across the river. Those were the ones I liked the most.

A postcard.

That's what I'd send my father.

As for the message—

Along Kanawha Street,
Charlston, W. V.

Chesapeake & Ohio Depot, Charleston, W. Va.

Dear Father,
  Grandpa is no longer against you.

Plant a seed. See what grows. If my father wrote back and things seemed peaceable, then I'd send him my photograph.

As I left the bookshop with my globe and my postcards, I paused, caught up in Grandpa's caution.

Don't spend it on trifles.

Thump-thump.

I thought about my photographs I still had to pay for. I thought about my hat. My globe. The postcards. Though I still had several silver dollars and change on me, I wondered if I had done wrong.

Pshaw! a strong, sure voice exclaimed. *These are not trifles. These are things dear to you!*

I smiled. And on my way I went.

- - - - -

At Friedman's, that same girl was in the window. When she saw me, she smiled and waved. I stopped, waved back.

She had made changes to that mannequin in the peach satin gown. Now she had on long black gloves and a broad-brimmed black satin hat, cocked to one side.

The girl was pinning something on the mannequin's shoulder. When she stepped back, I did a double take, peered closer.

The pin was a dragonfly.

They are one of God's joys to the world. Sign of a better day coming! Of new beginnings!

The way the sunlight hit the pin—copper body, red eyes, front wings green, back wings blue—I felt like shimmershine!

Then and there, I decided to stop being scared of dragonflies. So I'd always have a reminder, I went inside and purchased that pin.

After that, I had one more stop in mind. Over to Kanawha Street and down by the river. To guess which was Aunt Tilley's welcoming tree.

Then, I thought better. *Save that for another day.*

Dusk was coming on. And after all, I no longer wondered about Aunt Tilley's last wish. I knew.

I also knew Grandpa would be home by now. I could see him pacing the porch or in the sitting room playing checkers with himself, but looking at his pocket watch every other minute.

I didn't want Grandpa to worry.

With a jumping-jack joy over my first on my own, I headed straight home. To my family.

GATES ART GALLERY.   CHARLESTON, W. VA.

Jacob ‖ Janie

Able Carter ‖ Comfort

Matilda (Tilley) ‖ Double Carter (Dub)

Eula Carter

Matthias Carter

Victoria Carter

Richard Carter ‖ Cora Scott

Thomas Carter (Tophat)

James Carter

Matilda Carter

Peonia Carter ‖ Luke Morris

Peonia Morris

Penelope Morris

London Smith ‖ Bessie

Peter Morris

Jacob Fuller ‖ Mamie Smith

Elijah Smith ‖ Rosetta Maple

Wade Fuller

Emma Smith

Ambertine Fuller

Clare Smith

Lena Smith

Delana's Family

- Delana's grandparents' generation
- Delana's parents' generation
- Delana's generation
- Highlighted names are characters that appear in photos

Note: Like Grandpa, many enslaved people did not have last names but chose ones to their liking when freedom came.

Alexander Hall —— Carrie

Lavinia (Viney)

Alexander Hall, Jr.

Mahala Hall

Jonathan Wright —— Mary

Patience Wright —— Rufus Dowd

Selia Dowd

Solomon Dowd

Sophronia Dowd

Sillah Dowd

Rachel Wright

Samuel Hannibal (Grandpa) —— Delia Wright

Lucinda Hannibal

Lucas Hannibal

Samuel Hannibal, Jr.

William Burkett —— Ana Miles

Joline Hannibal —— Jordan Burkett

Delana Burkett

Author's Note

Over the years, I've come to collect old books, old newspapers and magazines, antique ink bottles, pre-1964 U.S. coins, and, yes, photographs, most of them well over one hundred years old. (And I wouldn't put it past me to start collecting antique globes now.)

When I started collecting photographs, I wasn't picky about much—often not even about condition. Ditto on type. I adored the little 2^{1}/$_{2}$×4-inch *carte-de-visite* (which Aunt Tilley calls "card visits") as much as I did larger photographs mounted on card stock, such as the 4^{1}/$_{2}$×6^{1}/$_{2}$-inch cabinet card (so called because they were often displayed in cabinets). I also picked up images produced on metal—tintypes (also known as melainotypes and ferrotypes).

Whatever the condition, whatever the type or size, it was most always the faces that entranced me.

Did he have a love for the sea? I let myself guess about a very proud-looking man with derby and walking stick.

What was she thinking about? A loss? A longing? A secret? I wondered of an elderly woman wearing a hat with a white feather and seated in a chair that brought to my mind a throne.

What did she want out of life? I asked as I studied the gaze of a girl who had her photograph taken around the turn of the last century at Gates Art Gallery in Charleston, West Virginia.

Finding Family was born of my wonderings about the faces I collected over the years: people whose real identities are mysteries to me.

So, yes, the photographs in *Finding Family* are of people who once walked the earth, but their stories— names, personalities, kinships—all fiction. With one exception: *Heroes of the Colored Race.* Nothing fanciful here, and this 1881 lithograph isn't from my collection, but from the Library of Congress.

Just as I created stories for the photographs, I took other liberties as well. For instance, Adena's neighborhood, the Hollow, is real, but not as near to Delana's home as I suggest. Two, while the postcards are from the early 1900s, their original messages have been changed.

Still, more often than not, in context and setting I have been faithful to history as much as possible. The quick sketch of Martin Delany's life is no fabulation, but Aunt Tilley does have trouble with his sons' names ("Alexander Doomas" should be Alexandre Dumas and "Two Cent" should be Toussaint L'Ouverture). In a similar vein, Aunt Tilley's "Melungin" is another person's "Melungeon," a once-derogatory name for a people of mixed ethnicity who typically lived in northeast Tennessee, western Virginia, eastern Kentucky, and elsewhere in the South: a people about whom you can read in memoirs and history books.

As for other matters of history, in introducing Delana to another of my heroes, Frances Ellen Watkins Harper, I used the 1891 edition of Harper's book *Sketches of Southern Life*. And yes, the Honorable Blanche K. Bruce really used the word "dude." His speech and everything else Delana learns about the Tri-State Emancipation Day celebration where her parents met are straight out of the September 23, 1891, *Wheeling Intelligencer.*

History inspired other aspects of the book, too. The

interior of Delana's home is based on that of Frederick Douglass's last home, in Anacostia. Fascinated as I am by black strivers of the nineteenth century—especially those who came "up from slavery"—bits of Booker T. Washington's life went into the making of Grandpa. My awareness of another once-enslaved high achiever, William Johnson, the "Barber of Natchez," triggered my decision on Grandpa's trade and that of his mentor/liberator, Hannibal Watson. As for their relationship, that sprang from the knowledge that when it comes to actual cases of blacks holding other blacks in bondage, there's often more than meets the eye.

On one last source of inspiration: when I sent Delana off to Gates's place, in the forefront of my mind was an early 1900s photograph of the Washington, D.C., studio of the pioneering female photographer Frances Benjamin Johnston.

So in the making of *Finding Family* I had the great thrill of combining my passion for history with my wonderings about long-ago lives: the millions of everyday people from the past who experienced problems with peers, traumas, and dilemmas, and in the end life-lifting revelations like we do today; people who are footnotes in history books—or not in history books at all.

Thankfully, in museums and historical societies, in libraries and private collections, we have people's diaries, family Bibles, handicrafts, letters, and other artifacts—like photographs. Such treasures not only give us insights into history but also allow our imaginations to take flight.

As for your life, I hope that you will take good care of artifacts from it, along with your family stories. A century into the future, what you have left behind may very well be prized by a writer working on a book of nonfiction. Or fiction.

Acknowledgments

I cannot thank you enough, my editor, Michelle H. Nagler: for embracing this project from the start; for your adept direction; for your superb sensibilities; and for all that terrific energy. Stay relentless.

To other wonderful people in the Bloomsbury family—in editorial, design, production, and post-production—thank you so much for all your great work: Caroline Abbey, Diana Blough, Regina Castillo, Melanie Cecka, Jill Davis, Danielle Delaney, Beth Eller, Alexei Esikoff, Katie Fee, Beth Jordan, Melissa Kavonic, Donna Mark, Patricia McHugh, Vanessa Nuttry, and Deb Shapiro.

For your feedback on the manuscript, thank you: Sharon Franklin, librarian at Andrew Lewis Middle

School, Salem, VA; Susan Hess, retired New York City public school librarian, and Bobby Thomas. For reading *and* for all your consultations and education on antique photographs, thank you, Greg French of Greg French Early Photography in Jamaica Plain, Massachusetts.

Bless your heart, Joyce Hansen, for reading, too, and for that early support and encouragement when I called you up lost and in a panic. I'll never forget your generosity and your wisdom words.

Thanks are also due to the good people at Omniterrum, in Lynchburg, Virginia, for the assist in my research on antique globes; to Eleanor Beckner at the McDowell Public Library in Welch, West Virginia, for help with Cucumber; to Amy Kastigar at Ohio County Public Library, in Wheeling, West Virginia, for clarifying some things about the Emancipation Day article in the *Wheeling Intelligencer*; to Richard "Casey" James for writing *In the Hollow* and Anthony Kinser, Sr., of the West Virginia Center for African American Art & Culture for making the connection.

And to my agent, Jennifer Lyons, thank you a thousand times for *everything* that you do.

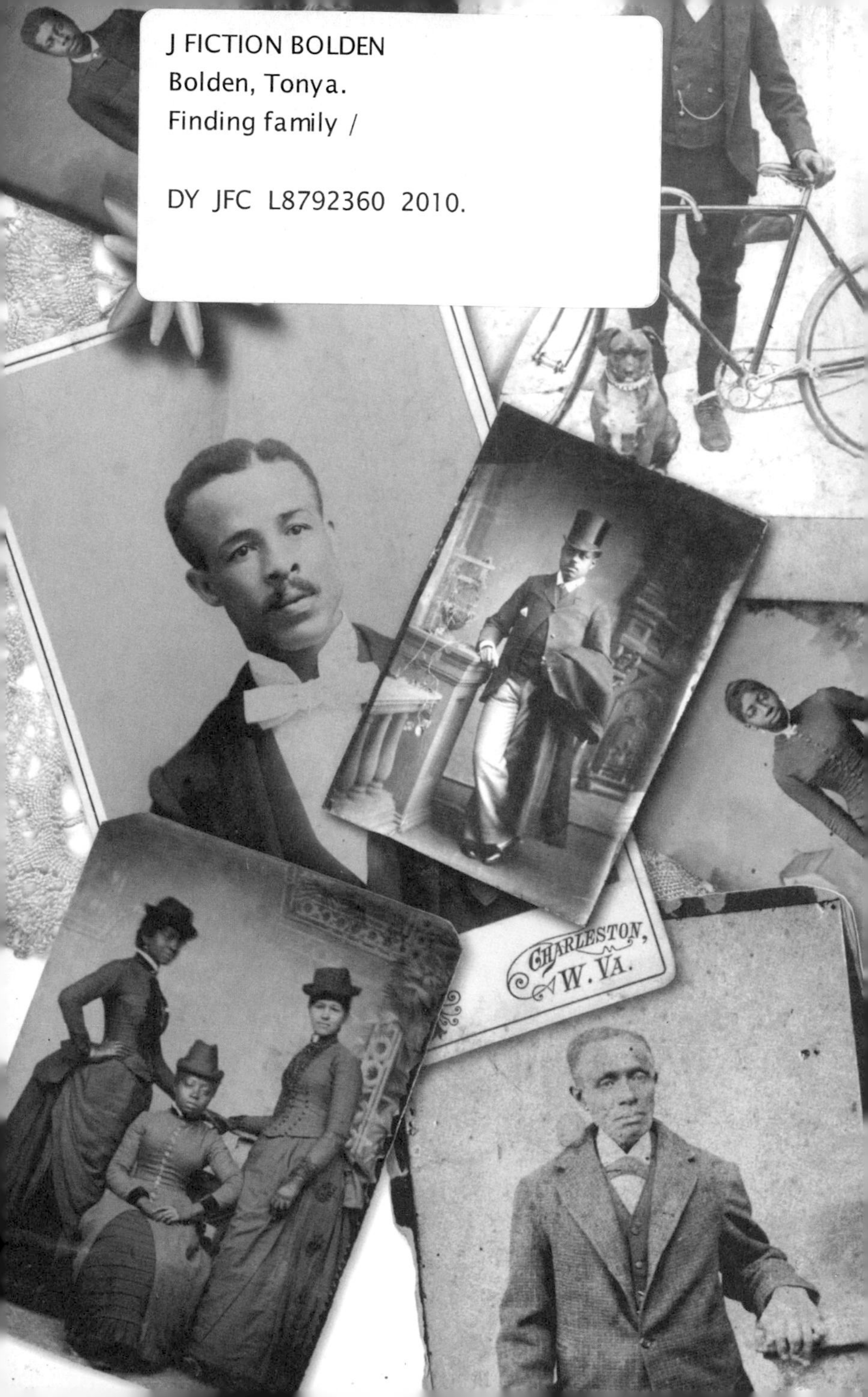
CHARLESTON,
W. VA.